The Dirty Divorce Part 3

A NOVEL BY
MISS KP

Life Changing Books in conjunction with Power Play Media
Published by Life Changing Books
P.O. Box 423 Brandywine, MD 20613

Library of Congress Cataloging-in-Publication Data;

www.lifechangingbooks.net
13 Digit: 978-1934230305
10 Digit: 1-934230308

Dedication

To my prince, my son, Mateo Gabriel. You've been with me throughout this Dirty Divorce Movement. Mommy loves you to pieces!

Acknowledgements

First of all, I would like to thank God for all of the blessings. This journey has been more than what I could've ever imagined. Three books in one year…wow! I couldn't have done it without my family, friends, and readers. Without your support this wouldn't have been possible. Kami and Mateo, Mommy loves you so much. I work hard every day for you both. You give me purpose in this world and I'm always a mother first. Love you Doodie and Jordan. Rodney, what a year!! It's been crazy, but God is good. To my mother, Lita Gray, I love you dearly. To my sister, Mia, this year defined the true meaning of sisterhood. Jawaun and Cornell, you da best! Daddy, I love you and I don't mind having some of my Daddy's ways, it's made me the no-nonsense woman I am today. Sydni, Javone, EB and Brent, love you guys. Toya, Pam (Gill), Poo, Latrease, Letitia, Sam, Indiah, Shana, Donovan, Frank, Whitey, Detrick, Rob, and Jermaine, thanks for being my friends to the end.

To Leslie Allen and Tressa aka-Azarel, I love you guys! Thanks for pushing me and making this dream possible. To my test readers and LCB family…we da best!

There are many loved ones who have passed on that I wish were here to witness my dreams come true, so I would like to thank them for touching my life. Aunt Shirley, I feel like you helped me find the creative girl inside of me. You always believed in me and I miss you so much. Big Ma, I lost you, the only grandmother I've ever known while writing this book and I want you to know that I will love you forever. Nicky "Coach Lynch", my cousin, you have touched so many people's lives and have definitely left your mark on the world. I miss you and wish that you were still here.

Many thanks again to everyone that I thanked in Part 1 and Part 2…This one is for the readers and bookstores (The Literary Joint, Urban Knowledge, Black and Nobel, Borders, Barnes and Nobel) and anyone else that have supported me through this journey. AAMBC thanks for awarding me with Urban Book of the Year. I have posted a handful of reviews from Amazon.com to show love to the fans! If I could fit all of your comments I would.

Over 75 FIVE STAR REVIEWS
THE DIRTY DIVORCE PART 1 AMAZON REVIEWS
Reviews have been published in original unedited versions

A great Urban novel, May 27, 2010 By **R. Mobley "Kindle Reader"** (Washington DC) Within the first 10 pages the reader was drawn into the arising drama. This book was definitely was a page turner. After reading the coldest winter ever, I searched the Urban book shelf for a book that was similar, but to no avail, until The Dirty Divorce landed on my Kindle. Looking forward in reading the continuation "The Dirty Divorce 2"

July 20, 2010 By **Lesa Jones E.J "~~Lesa!~~"** (Milwaukee, WI)Well now waiting for part 2 so I can finish this story. Great book overall from the start to the end. Great book can't wait for part 2 :)

LISA IS THE BADDEST B!, May 31, 2010 By **Yvette** (Virginia) - This book was sooo good. I thought Lisa was the sweet wife that would just keep taking and taking, but she came back hard on Rich. She got gansta on them all. If you like sex, drugs, drama and violence, this book is for you. I could not put it down. I can't wait for part 2. Miss KP did the damn thing on this one, it was sooo good.

OMG!!!, August 13, 2010 By **D. Prophete "Divas of Literature"** (Charlotte, NC) - All I can say is...there are very few books that I feel the need to review but THIS BOOK was crazy!! I never even heard of this author but I am so glad I stumbled across this book...and thanks to the reviews I decided to give it a shot...It's been a long time since an author was able to grab my attention from the very beginning and hold my attention to the very ending leaving my mouth wide open and devastated that I have to wait until part two!! I can't see anyone that would be disappointed with this read. It was definitely a different kind of street novel. Loved it!!!!! You go girlllllll.

Great Reading!, August 4, 2010 By **Tina** Once I got started reading this book I could not put it down. This story has to be true....there is no way someone can put this down on paper as a fiction story. The last 10 minutes of the read had me hanging off the edge of my chair. After the tour de france I was left hanging...WHAT..cliff hanger! OMG...I can not wait for part 2!

OMG, July 30, 2010 By **Poetik77** Okay, I just finished The Dirty Divorce and already I am hungry for the sequel. If I could have given this book 10 stars I would have. This book was good from the beginning to the end. If you haven't purchased this book, RUN to your nearest bookstore and purchase it now!!! OMG...GREAT book. Holding my breath until November for the sequel. Great JOB Miss KP.

TALK ABOUT A DIRTY DIVORCE" THIS IS IT!, July 28, 2010 By **LOVE2READ "TJ"** (HOME OF THE CRABS, MARYLAND) This book was off the hook on the 4th page. I couldn't put it down.

HOT!!!!!, August 19, 2010 By **Donna J. Booker "Donna Boo"**

THIS BOOK IS OFF DA CHAIN! CAN'T WAIT 4 THE SE-QUEL! GREAT ACTION & STORY LINE. LOVE HOW THE TIES THAT BIND ARE NEATLY DISPLAYED THAT BROUGHT ABOUT SUCH A CLIFF HANGER ENDING! READ THIS BOOK IN 4 HOURS!

Wow!, September 13, 2010 By **Shelia Little "S. Little"** (Charlotte, NC) I purchased this book because the reviews were excellent. I recently purchased the IPAD & was excited to get started downloading books. I didn't even know what the book was about. Miss KP certainly did her thing with this one; I can't wait until November for part 2.

They are about to get DOWN & DIRTY with this divorce!, August 30, 2010 By **K. Brown "Kamazing Poet"** (Bridgeport, CT) OMG!! This book was soooo blazing! It had me hooked from start to finish. Definitely a page turner

THE DIRTY DIVORCE PART 2 AMAZON REVIEWS

New Secrets & Drama...TOPS DIRTY DIVORCE 1, December 1, 2010 By **Laquita Adams "Book Store Owner and Critic"** (Maryland) - We finally have what we all have been waiting for and boy did Miss KP achieve what most authors dream of, A SMASHING PART 2 that will make you forget about all of the drama in part 1.

DJ(New Jersey), December 13, 2010- First of all I had so much trouble finding this book after complaining so much my cousin drove a hour away to a urban book store and got it, lets just say I owe him. I usually hate sequels because it's hard for me to remember what happen in the first one. This story just flowed and continued very easily. I loved all the twist and turns if you loved the first one you will love this one just as much.

Good Book, March 5, 2011 By **Reda** - This book is really good, it held my attention from beginning to end, my jaws dropped, my eyes bulged, heart sank, and the end has just blown my mind. I can't wait to read The Dirty

A MUST READ, January 15, 2011 By **Sharon J. Harris** **"sweetreader"** (Newark, NJ) - THE DIRTY DIVORCE 2 IS A THE BEST BOOK I READ IN THE NEW YEAR CAN'T WAIT FOR THE THIRD PART

Dirty Divorce, January 3, 2011 By **S. Colbert "Book Lover"** (California) This was a good read. If you want drama this is the book to read. I can't wait until Dirty Divorce 3 comes out.

Anticipating Dirty Divorce 3, December 29, 2010 By **MissKJ** -This book is a page turner from the beginning to end. Like most, I have been anticipating this sequel since it came out, so now the wait begins for Part 3.

DRAMA, DRAMA, DRAMA, AND MO DRAMA!!!!, December 27, 2010 By **Ms. Nett** (mo) - Lisa has really lost her damn mind! I won't go into details for those of you that haven't read it but don't sleep on this one! Great book!

OMG~, April 29, 2011 By **Nodrama** - This book is really another page turner. Lisa has turned out to be a monster but I guess Rich has done that. Miss KP is doing her thing & I love it! I am patiently awaiting book #3

OMG! From beginning to end (pt. 1 & 2), March 3, 2011 By **Myprsnlbzns**- I must say, I am blown away by Ms. KP. I was browsing through amazon for new authors with series, I came across Ms. KP. Since The Dirty Divorce 1 & 2 had 5 stars I decided to give it a try...and I'll be damned. I read both books in a matter of 48 hours flat, really no lie. Ms KP is definitely added to my favorite authors list. KP is just fabulous. I'm getting on her facebook train tonight, and becoming a KP groupie:-

) lol. Can't wait till May, for part 3.....please put it on kindle first.

As you can see, I'm overwhelmed by all the positive responses. I know part 3 wouldn't be possible if it weren't for the fans, so once again, I thank you from the bottom of my heart. Keep your reviews coming, I learn from you all.

Much luv & hugz!
Miss KP

www.miss-kp.com
www.twitter.com/misskpdc
www.facebook.com/misskpdc
www.lifechangingbooks.net

Chapter 1

Rich

This shit felt too perfect. Just like I wanted, the car was parked in a secluded spot, away from anyone else. The red eye comin' back from Vegas to Dulles Airport was just what I needed to make this happen. It was time to get paid. Besides, that bitch owed me big, so I needed to collect what was mine.

My rental car was parked outside the garage so I could easily roll out undetected. As I hid between her black Porshe Cayenne and the wall, I watched her strut toward the truck wit' dark sunglasses and five-inch heels lookin' like one of them Kardashian bitches.

Damn, does she have to look that good at five a.m. when I'm about to jack her for her bread, I thought.

The closer she got, I kept my eye on her monogrammed Louis Vuitton carry-on luggage. Gettin' in position wit' my black ski mask and Issey Miyake oil that I'd bought from a Muslim stand just to throw her off, it was time to make my move. I knew she wasn't totein' since she'd just gotten off the plane, so this shit was gonna be like takin' candy from a helpless child. Wit' my Desert Eagle in hand, I was ready to get back on top. Walkin' up behind her, I placed the gun directly on her spine.

"Get de fuck on de ground bitch!" I yelled in my fake Jamaican accent. I'd been workin' on the disguise for a while now.

Seconds later, I hit her wit' the butt of my gun, landin' the blow on her shoulder. Never was I a stick-up kid or some type of dude that came up off robbin' niggas, but I was desperate for cash and this was the come up I needed to get back on my feet. She instantly fell to the ground.

"You bitch-ass niggas always gotta go after a female. You ain't a real nigga!" she yelled.

The bitch was obviously in pain, but still tried to fight back. Once she scratched my neck, my anger instantly intensified.

"Oh, yeah bitch!" I cocked the gun back to let her ass know that I meant business. "You think this shit a joke!"

As my neck stung like hell I tried to stay focused and almost forgot about my Jamaican accent.

"Please don't shoot me, I'm a mother," she finally pleaded.

"I don't give a fuck if ya a mauder or not! Where de money at?" I reached down and grabbed her long hair.

I hadn't seen her in a while, so I noticed that she'd let her hair grow back which was good. I wasn't down wit' that fake-ass weave shit.

"I don't have any money. Here, take my car," she said, throwin' the keys.

"Bumboclot bitch, I don't want ya car, I want de money! I want it now or ya gonna die and ya kids won't have nobody!"

She paused for a moment. "It's in the suitcase." She handed the luggage over. "Take it, just don't hurt me."

Grabbin' her roughly between her legs I held onto her pussy as she squirmed, but cooperated. Lookin' sexy in one of those long maxi dresses, I couldn't resist feelin' her up.

"Ya know I would take ya pussy if I had da time."

"Please, don't, I'll give you whatever you want! I just need to go home to my babies!"

Although she was pleadin' for her life, the crazy part about it was that she'd yet to shed a single tear.

"Keep ya head down bitch!" I yelled, then kicked her in the mouth for tryin' to look up at me. "If de money not here, I'm gonna kill ya kids."

"It's there! It's there!" she screamed.

I threw her car keys over the wall so I would have enough time to get away.

"Bitch ya don't get up until ya count to five hundred. And don't try any funny business because my man is watchin' ya. If he sees ya get up sooner than I instructed, ya die. Got me?"

"Yes...yes," she said, holdin' her mouth.

She was bleedin' pretty bad, and when I looked down, I realized some of the blood had gotten on my New Balance sneakers.

Hoppin' over the concrete wall wit' the Louie luggage in hand, I looked around to see if anyone was watchin' before runnin' to my car that was in the hourly parkin' lot. As soon as I reached the rented Jeep Cherokee, I jumped inside and pulled off. I made sure to take the mask off before payin' the attendant, but also made sure not to look the old-lookin' man in his face. My plan had succeeded so far, so I didn't need him to get suspicious.

Hoppin' on I-66, I blasted my Drake CD and smiled. *It's gonna feel good to be back on top*, I thought to myself. I was tired of barely makin' it and as bad as I felt, I had to do what I had to do to survive.

Sorry I had to do that shit to you Marisol, but a nigga gotta eat.

There weren't many people on the road, so I actually made it home to my mother's house in less than forty minutes. Pullin' up in the driveway the anticipation was killin' me. I couldn't wait to find out how much bread I'd made out wit'. I put the luggage in a trash bag before gettin' out of the car just in case someone was watchin', then power walked up to the door. After walkin' inside, I ran up to my room takin' two steps at a time.

I felt somewhat bad for what I'd done, but then again that bitch was on her way back from doin' a deal that I helped her set up, so part of the money belonged to me anyway. I couldn't believe Marisol had let Renzo's punk-ass talk her out of dealin' wit' me. She shouldn't even be fuckin' wit' that nigga after what he did to Juan in the first place. That was sendin' me a 'money over fam' message. We didn't need Renzo to run this shit, but obviously that bitch felt otherwise, so fuck her. I was done wit' her anyway. If it wasn't for Marisol, Juan might've still been alive. Shit, she was lucky I hadn't killed her ass for that. Hell, she deserved an ass whoopin' for leavin' Denie on me and Lisa's doorstep alone. Her wounds would heal, but my son was gone and my daughter was probably messed up for life, so I had no remorse.

I was so happy that her nanny, Maria, had called me in a panic when she couldn't get in touch wit' Marisol. It was her who'd told me that Marisol was supposed to be on a red eye from Vegas and what airport her plane was due to land. Apparently, Mia was sick once again. I didn't understand why Maria thought Marisol could answer the phone while she was on the plane anyway, but was ecstatic for the information. After assurin' Maria that Marisol would be in touch as soon she landed, I made plans to make my move. I knew what that bitch was in Vegas about, and she wasn't about to get paid without me.

Dumpin' the luggage out of the trash bag, then onto the bed, I unzipped the bag that was filled wit' clothes. Tossin' all that shit out along wit' three pairs of shoes, I was startin' to think Marisol had lied until I finally came across a matchin' Louis Vuitton toiletry case. Once I opened it and saw four bundles of cash, I thought I'd hit the jackpot. However those thoughts quickly changed.

"What the fuck is this?" I asked starin' at the cash.

After openin' the first two bundles and countin', fifty, one-hundred dollar bills in each one, I knew the other stacks were exactly the same. All the fuck I got out of this shit was a lousy twenty g's.

Grabbin' the luggage, I turned that shit upside, hopin' some more money would fall out. I even tapped the bottom a few times, but nothin' came out but a tube of Mariosl's fuckin' lipstick. What the fuck was I supposed to do wit' this little bit of cash? I'd hit that bitch off for some short shit! I wondered if Marisol had done somethin' wit' the rest of the dough before I got to her. Turnin' around, I took my fist and rammed it straight through the drywall before goin' back downstairs to take a shot.

This was some bullshit for real.

Chapter 2

Marisol

My face felt like it was on fire. At that moment I wish I could've been strong, but it was too late as tears of anger streamed down my cheeks. When I found out who was responsible for this shit, they were definitely gonna die of a slow, miserable death for violating me. The last thing I wanted was for the streets to think I was weak. Now, it's a must that I stay strapped at all times.

As I crawled closer to my purse and picked up all my things that were scattered all over the ground, I wondered how the hell I was gonna get home. I wasn't in any condition to go searching for my keys. Just when I felt defeated, I remembered my spare key being in a magnetic case under the car. That was one good thing about Carlos; he trained me to always have a spare key compartment in all my vehicles and even at the house in case of an emergency, especially since I was forever losing my keys.

How the hell did I allow somebody to catch me slipping?

After all the things Carlos taught me so I would be prepared for a moment like this, I still got robbed. I could honestly say that for once I wasn't paying attention to my surroundings, which in this game was a no-no. Picking my sore body off the ground, I walked toward the left rear tire, reached under the car and grabbed the case. After retrieving the spare key, the first thing I did when I finally got inside my truck was pull the visor down.

I can't believe that muthafucka busted my lip," I said, eyeing the damage. Even my front tooth felt loose.

There was no way my girls could see me like this, so my intentions were to head to Carlos' old stash house in Clinton to get myself cleaned up and make sure that bastard hadn't hit that spot up while I was out of town.

It was a shame that Rich was the only person I really could call to help me right now, but I needed him. I had to swallow my pride and let him know what was going on despite the fact that we still weren't on good terms. Ever since I'd revealed that Denie was my daughter, along with Juan being murdered, and me still dealing with Renzo, things hadn't been the same between us. I could admit that it was foul for me to keep the Denie secret away from him all these years, but I had nothing to do with Juan getting killed. Hell, I didn't even know that he was a snitch. However, informant or not, I loved Juan and never wanted to see him get hurt. As crazy as these streets were, Rich could've been next in line to take a hit, so I had to warn him. Maybe this would bring us closer together.

I picked up my phone and dialed Rich's number, but he didn't answer. I had to be persistent in this case, so I called again. This time he answered.

"Hello," Rich whispered. It sounded as if he was half asleep.

"Rich, wake up! Somebody just robbed me!" I yelled hysterically.

"What? Where are you?"

"I'm about to leave Dulles airport. That bitch-ass nigga robbed me in the parking garage when I was about to get into my truck."

"Damn, that's fucked up. So, it was just one dude? Did you see anybody else?"

"Yeah, it was just one guy. He said somebody else was with him, but I think his ass was lying," I informed.

"Did he hurt you?" Rich asked.

"I'm a little sore and swollen, but I'll live. If my front tooth comes out from him kicking me though, I'm gonna fucking lose it!"

"Shit could've been worse. At least he didn't try to take your pussy or nothin'."

I paused for a moment. "Damn, that was really nice to say."

"My bad. What did he get?"

"All he got was some short change. I was on my way back from Vegas. I was actually out there tryin' to take care of that deal you and I put together a while ago, but I never got a chance to do anything. I had to leave early because I got a call about Mia being sick. Shit, all he got was my shopping and play money for real," I stated. "He threatened my kids, Rich. I'm gonna kill that muthafucka when I find out who it is!"

"Damn, who do you think it was? Maybe he knows somethin'."

"He sounded Jamaican. I wonder if it was David and them from Uptown. But then again how would they have known I was gonna be at the airport? Dulles airport at that?"

At that moment, I began to rack my brain as to who knew my whereabouts, and then it hit me…Maria. She was the only one who knew I was coming back.

"I have no idea. So, what do you need me to do?" Rich questioned.

"Nothing I guess. I just wanted to let you know what was going on. I wouldn't want a nigga to catch you off guard. Where are you anyway?"

"I'm not in town right now, but I'll be back tomorrow. We can meet up if you still wanna talk."

I displayed a slight smile. It had been a few months since

I'd seen him.

"Okay. I need to figure out who's responsible for this shit. They might be connected to what happened to Carlos."

"Damn, you right. Well I'ma holler at you when I get back in town. Watch your back and make sure nobody is followin' you."

"I will."

****

It's always something, I thought to myself as I hung up the phone. As if I didn't have enough shit going on right now, I'd just agreed to meet Jade's brother, Javier, later that evening. With the way my day started, I wasn't in the mood to meet with anybody, but the urgency in his voice had me concerned. He thought he was slick. Didn't he know I could see straight through his bullshit? I knew his ass didn't want to meet me for nothing. With the recession along with a drought in the streets, I'm sure the thirsty nigga just wanted a quick come up. Even though we'd done business together in the past, I wasn't about to add him to the payroll though, especially since my relationship with his sister was strained. I hadn't heard from that bitch in months. She'd proven her friendship when she turned her back on me, so Jade could definitely kiss my ass. However, despite my personal feeling for his sister, I was gonna try my best to keep that shit separate from business.

After stopping by the stash house to check on things, I drove around for almost two hours trying to get myself together. The last thing I wanted was for me to be upset when I got home to my girls. Blowing off as much steam as possible was the best way to put me in a good 'mommy' role, so I made sure my mind was clear before pulling up to my house.

However, as soon as I placed my truck in park, there was something that had me paralyzed and I couldn't get out. The May weather had finally turned over and I admired the rose bushes that Carlos and I planted when we first bought our house. As I sat in my truck and peered through the tinted windows, I felt a sense of guilt. I wondered what Carlos would think of me now, knowing how I'd betrayed him. Sleeping with his brother was one thing, but letting Rich father my first born would've definitely been unforgivable. As a mother to Carmen and Mia, I'm also sure he wouldn't have liked the way I'd abandoned Denie and allowed Lisa to raise her.

Wondering if he would've tried to take my youngest daughters away from me, my thoughts suddenly drifted to Mia. I couldn't believe she was sick was again. Listening to Maria tell me about her symptoms, I hoped her Leukemia hadn't returned. If that was the case, if she had to go to one of the best doctor's in the country, I was gonna do everything in my power to make sure we beat that shit once and for all. Sure…I was a horrible mother with Denie, but considered myself an excellent one now.

When I finally got out of the car and walked through the door, I was instantly greeted by my two little rug rats. I automatically felt uplifted.

"Mommy, Mommy!" they yelled enthused and excited to see me.

It was only eight o'clock and Carmen already had tons of energy.

"Hello Mommy's pumpkins. How are you?"

All three of us embraced in a huge hug.

"Good! What's in the bags Mommy? Are those gifts for us?" Carmen yelled.

It was sad, but true. I'd spoiled these girls so much that they expected gifts every time I came home. That was my way of covering up my absence, it was my guilt.

"Mommy, what happened to your mouth?" Carmen asked.

"Oh, it's nothing. Mommy just had a small accident, that's all." I turned to my other daughter. "Mia, honey how are you feeling?"

"I'm not feeling good, Mommy. My stomach and my head hurts."

"She's been complaining for a couple of days now, Ms. Marisol," Maria answered.

When I looked at my nanny, thoughts about her being the only person to know my whereabouts flooded my mind like a river. Although I'd spent hours to calm myself down, now I was pissed off all over again.

I pointed toward the dining room. "Maria, can I speak to you for a second?"

"Sure."

As soon as we walked a few feet away from the girls, I instantly got up in her face. I was so close, I'm sure she could smell the remains of the Starbucks Cinnamon Latte on my breath.

"Now, listen to me, Maria and listen good. I like you and all, but trust me, I'll send your ass back to Cuba in a fucking box if you lie to me. Did you tell anyone where I was?"

Her eyes were the size of watermelons. "No, Ms. Marisol. I tell no one where you are," she replied in her broken English.

"Are you sure?" I yelled.

"Yes, Ms. Marisol…please. I tell no one. Please don't fire me." She clutched her hands as if her ass was about to pray.

Figuring that she was probably telling the truth, I decided to let it go. "Don't ever tell anyone where I am when I go out of town or when I'm coming back. Only you and the kids should know that," I lectured.

She shook her head. "Of course."

When we turned around to walk back toward the girls, Maria tapped my shoulder.

"Umm, Ms. Marisol, I didn't want to bother you while you were away, but I'm worried about Denie. She's very mean to the little ones. Also, I think she's been smoking in her room. A strong smell is coming from under her door."

"Oh really? Well, I'll handle Denie. Can you take the girls to the playroom and let them open their gifts? After that, get Mia ready. I'm gonna take her over to Children's Hospital, so Dr. Friedman can take a look at her before my meeting tonight."

"Yes, Ms. Marisol."

As I climbed the stairs to Denie's room, I took a deep breath and prepared myself for the conversation that needed to happen. I knew that she was envious of the girls subconsciously, but acted as if it didn't faze her on the surface. I had to be careful with her though; she was scorned and capable of anything, especially with what she'd done to Lisa. Who would've thought that my daughter would be capable of trying to poison someone? Even what she'd done to Rich was quite clever. After everything went down a couple of months ago, Rich and I thought it was best that Denie stayed with me so we could try and rebuild our relationship as mother and daughter. She and Rich were like oil and vinegar now, and couldn't seem to get along. It seemed weird that she was more upset with Rich than me. She refused to even speak to him sometimes. Leaving her with Rich and Lisa had obviously done more harm than good, but that still didn't give her a reason to act like a bitch toward her sisters.

She might've gotten away with that kind of behavior with Lisa, but not me. That shit wasn't gonna fly in my house…daughter or not. The closer I got to the door I could hear go-go music and Denie's constant giggling. Figuring she was on the phone with some knuckle head, I knocked two times. Technically, she was grown and I didn't want to violate her privacy.

"What do you want Maria?" she yelled.

"Denie open the door, it's Marisol!" I yelled back. I couldn't believe she spoke to Maria with such disrespect.

Seconds later, Denie cracked the door open. "Wassup, I didn't know you were home." She seemed surprised and caught off guard.

"I just got here. What are you doing, open the door."

"No, this is my room. You just can't come in here."

"Who the hell are you talking to? Get out the way!"

At that moment, I knew something was going on. Pushing the door open, my eyes widened as I looked at Denie's barely dressed body along with some dude in her bed with gold teeth. The room reeked of weed and sex.

"Damn, baby, your momma fine as shit," the ghetto-ass nigga chimed in.

"What the fuck is going on in here? Get the hell out my house!" I pointed to the Lil' Wayne looking dude with piercing eyes.

"He's not going anywhere. Last time I checked, I was nineteen years old," Denie shot back.

Just like I'd done with Maria, I stepped up to her face…real close.

"Denie, don't fuck with me. I can't believe you're actually smoking weed and fucking some loser-ass nigga while my two babies are downstairs. If you wanna be that damn disrespectful, then I suggest you get your own spot or go back to live with Rich. Trust me, I won't have any problems kicking your ass out." I looked at the dude one last time. "Besides, you need to step your game up if you giving out free pussy. He looks broke." I walked back toward the door, then turned around. "He got five minutes to get out."

"Fuck you, bitch. I got mad paper!" he replied.

Immediately, I snapped and went straight in my room to get my gun. I had to show both of them I wasn't the bitch to fuck with. After being robbed earlier, I wasn't about to be disrespected in my own damn home. It took me a minute since my room was all the way on the other side of the house, but when I returned it was obvious they'd taken me for a joke. Now, Denie had the nerve to be sitting beside him with a smile on her face.

Heated, I cocked my nickel plated .9mm back and pointed it at that fool who thought he was running shit. For him to have so much mouth as soon as he saw the firearm aimed at his chest, the bitch in him instantly came out.

"Like I said, you got five muthafucking minutes, no my bad…now you got two minutes to get the fuck out my house. And Denie if you got a problem with it, you can go with him," I said.

Denie instantly switched up. "Jamal, you gotta go."

Jumping out of the bed, he grabbed his clothes along with his shoes and fake-ass jewelry, then ran to the door. To my surprise, he at least had on some boxers.

"You crazy as hell lady!" Jamal yelled as he ran down the steps that led to the back of the house half-dressed.

One mistake I'd obviously made was giving Denie the suite with the private entrance. Now, that decision was coming back to bite me.

That's what I get for trying to be nice when she first moved in, I thought.

Once I heard the back door slam, I turned toward Denie again. "Let's get something straight right now. There's only one head bitch in this house and that's me. Not to mention, you don't pay any fucking bills around here, therefore, you have no say so. You will respect my house and my rules if you wanna stick around. Do I make myself clear?"

"Stop treating me like I'm a little girl. I'm grown. I thought you were different. You're no different from Rich or Lisa? All of you hate me. I wish I was never born!"

"Denie, you can try and lay that guilt trip shit on me all you want, but it's not gonna work. I'm sorry for what I did, but at the same time I thought that was best for you. Now, when you live on your own that's when you're grown to me and can do whatever you want."

"But…"

"Let me finish. There are two little girls in this house who now look up to you as a big sister, so you've gotta make better choices. There's a lot on my plate right now, and I don't need to be worrying about you bringing random dudes in my damn house. Don't you understand that you could be a mark to get to me through my enemies? If you're not careful, I could lose the empire Carlos and I worked so hard to build."

I'd already slipped up earlier, so I didn't need her fucking up as well.

Denie looked at me and nodded her head. "I can respect that. I don't want you to look at me as a charity case. If you want me to leave, then I will."

"Denie, I'm not asking you to leave. I just need you to respect my wishes, that's all."

She paused for a moment. "I understand. Sorry about Jamal."

"I'm not about to say no problem because it is a problem. Just don't let it happen again." I walked over to the ashtray on her nightstand that contained a half-smoked blunt and picked it up. "And get rid of this, too. The only person allowed to smoke weed in this house is me."

Chapter 3

Marisol

After returning back from the hospital with Mia and taking a quick nap, it was time for me to meet with Javier. Completely drained after finding out that my baby's Leukemia had more than likely returned, I really didn't feel like leaving the house, but also didn't wanna go back on my word. Besides, I was becoming even more curious about what he wanted anyway.

Jumping in the shower, the hot, soothing water was just what I needed. With the day I'd experienced, my muscles were beyond tense and since I didn't have time for my daily workout, hopefully the shower would provide me some type of therapeutic massage.

When I stepped out a few minutes later, I wrapped up in my Victoria Secret's Pink robe, then sat at my vanity before running across a picture of me and Carlos back in the day. It's crazy because Rich was the one who'd taken the picture. We'd gone on vacation to Aruba with him and Lisa before I got pregnant with Carmen. Looking at how happy we seemed, the guilt that I carried started to take a toll on me again.

Carlos is probably turning over in his grave, I thought to myself.

It was history repeating itself. What made me any different from Uncle Renzo for what he'd done to his brother or even Rich? No matter how it was dissected, it was all betrayal.

When I looked in the mirror I stared at myself as tears formed in my eyes. However, instead of becoming emotional this time, I immediately wiped my face before getting myself together. In a sense there was no need to keep crying about the past, what's done was done. I couldn't erase anything.

After pulling my hair back in a ponytail, I applied some concealer to the top of my lip to try and hide my battle scar. I then put on some mineral foundation before doing a quick, natural smoky eye for my lids. My hair was definitely in need of some TLC. With Renzo locked up, and handing the business over to me, my life had never been busier. I'd never gone this long without getting my highlights done, and needed to get in someone's chair ASAP.

Before I put my clothes on, I texted Javier and told him to meet me at Dave and Busters inside White Flint Mall. Since I didn't know what this meeting was about, I wanted to keep it casual so he wouldn't get the wrong impression. Dinner at some restaurant would've forced us to stare into each other's eyes the entire time, and I didn't want that.

Slipping on my J Brand skinny jeans, I also put on a white James Pearse wife beater, along with some red Valentino flip flops. Even though my red Chanel bag and diamond cross didn't necessarily say casual, I needed to look like money at all times no matter what. It also didn't matter that I'd gotten robbed earlier. As a woman in this game money was the one thing that always guaranteed respect. I had to let these dudes know that there was a lot more to me than just a pretty face. I could never look like I'd fallen off, which would be a sure sign of weakness.

After kissing each of the girl's goodbye, I let Maria know that I would be out for a while and informed her to keep an eye on Denie. I also told her to call me if that nigga, Jamal, showed back up. If he felt bold and wanted to come back to my house again, this time things weren't gonna end so peacefully.

Once I jumped in my new Range Rover Sport, I slowly pulled out of the driveway. I had no idea what possessed me to buy another SUV since the Porshe was only a year old, but when I bought Denie her Range Rover a few weeks ago, it was so hot I had to have a white one for myself.

Driving down GW Parkway, I reflected back on the conversation between me and Mia's doctor earlier that day. Thinking all her pain was due to an infection, he'd prescribed my baby some antibiotics and wanted her to get tons of rest. He also informed me that Mia's Leukemia had more than likely returned, but wouldn't be sure until the test results came back. My stomach turned flips every time I thought about the cancer no longer being in remission. Thinking back to when I was pregnant with both Mia and Carmen, the doctors asked me both times if I wanted to bank their cord blood in case of an emergency, and I declined. At that time, who would've thought that my daughter would get sick? Now, I was at a loss. Still mourning my husband, I didn't know what I would do if I ever lost my daughter, too.

Moments later, I turned up the radio when the song, *Adore* by Prince came on. This song definitely reminded me of Carlos, when things were good. Feeling like an emotional roller coaster, I wanted so badly to pull the truck over and cry my eyes out. No matter how strong I tried to be, there was so much on my mind lately. But there was no sense in crying. Tears certainly weren't gonna bring him back.

Since there was limited parking, I pulled up to the mall's valet parking and got my ticket. Javier had text me ten minutes ago to let me know that he'd already arrived. After making my way up to the top floor and walking inside, I immediately spotted Javier over by the pool tables. He definitely looked like money.

Maybe he doesn't need me after all, I suddenly thought.

Javier and Jade were twins, but he was a lot darker than she was. Even though he seemed to have lost a ton of weight, his cocoa complexion, midnight-black, curly hair and tall frame still made him attractive. Actually, he was finer today than I'd ever remembered in the past. He was definitely a smaller version of Malik from the BET show, *The Game*.

"What's up, Javier, it's been a while?" I greeted him with a hug.

He smelled so damn good, I could tell how sexually frustrated I was after getting a slight tingle between my thighs.

"Hey, Marisol. Damn, Ma, you lookin' good as usual," he flirted in his New York accent.

"I see you've either been in the gym or you're on a crack diet," I joked.

"Real funny, I see you still a jokester. I've been takin' care of myself eatin' right, that's all."

"Well, whatever you're doing your ass could definitely bottle it up and sell it. Shit, it looks like you lost a good fifty pounds. It looks good on you though."

"Thanks. That means a lot comin' from you."

Growing up, Javier always had a crush on me, but since we were like family he never acted on it. We made our way to the bar area, grabbed a high cocktail table, and ordered drinks.

"So, Javier, what's up?" I got right to the point. We'd already spent enough time bullshitting.

"The first thing I wanted to talk to you about is Jade. What happened?"

"Javier, if Jade sent you here to try and talk to me, you're wasting your time. I haven't heard from her in months. And I don't..."

He instantly cut me off. "Yo' Marisol, my sister is dead! That's what I'm here to talk to you about. This ain't about business, this shit is personal."

My mouth flew open. "What do you mean she's dead? What happened? When?"

"Her body was found in a vacant buildin' in West Baltimore a few weeks ago. Well, actually her remains were found."

"A few weeks ago? Why didn't you tell me this sooner? Why are you just telling me this now?" I immediately felt bad about all the shit I'd been talking about her.

"Marisol, I've been tryin' to call you ever since Jade went missin', but you never hit me back. The last time anybody saw her was right before your husband's memorial service."

"Oh my God, are you serious?" I questioned in disbelief.

"Yeah. At first the fam wasn't that worried because Jade was known to disappear wit' dudes on a regular basis, especially after she met that nigga, Rich. But after a week or so went by, and she still hadn't called my mom, that's when we started to get concerned," Javier replied. "I tried to call you right after they found her remains. I even tried a few times after her private funeral last Saturday, but again you didn't answer. You're one hard woman to get in touch wit'. This ain't some shit you just leave on a voicemail."

"I'm so sorry, Javier. I've been dealing with a lot since Carlos died, so that was probably why I never answered. I can't believe this."

"Me either. I'm still in shock."

"Do you all have any leads on what happened?" I asked.

"Well, that's why I'm here. The autopsy showed that Jade was shot in her mouth wit' a .45, so we at least know how she died. I just need to know who did that shit. After Carlos' memorial she called me hysterical. She said that she feared for her life."

"For what?"

"Apparently Jade had somethin' on Rich, but she wouldn't tell me what it was. That shit had her shook though. I mean Marisol I'd never seen that side of my sister before. You know how she was. She was never scared of anybody, but ever since she started datin' Rich, she hadn't been the same. She started actin' weird. I need answers. My sister was all I had. Man, I swear if Rich had somethin' to do wit' my sister bein' murdered, I swear…" Javier explained.

"Okay, let's not jump to any conclusions yet, Javier. I'm tired of all these empty accusations. Holler at me when you got some concrete proof," I said, then attempted to get up from the table.

"Well, maybe this is the evidence you need. Jade gave me this before she left town." He handed me a white envelope. "She made me promise her that I would never open it. Even if somethin' happened to her, she made me swear that you were the only one to open it. As you can see, I've kept my word."

I was in complete shock, especially knowing that Jade had disappeared right after Carlos' memorial. Instantly, visions of her running out after her outburst ran through my mind. I had no idea what was going to be revealed, so I decided to open it later.

"I wasn't prepared for you to tell me this. I think I'm gonna be sick. I gotta go." I got up from the table and threw a couple of twenties on the table.

"Yo' Marisol, wait a minute, there might be answers in there that reveals what happened to my sister!" Javier yelled.

"If it is, I'll be in touch," I quickly answered.

Making my way down the escalator and out the front door, I gave the valet guy my ticket then paced back and forth while waiting for my car. My mind raced with suspicion of what the envelope would reveal to me. Finally, after my truck pulled up a few minutes later, I quickly pulled out of the parking lot and made my way toward Rockville Pike. However, I didn't make it very far before the contents of the envelope flooded my thoughts. As I made a right on Tuckerman Street and pulled over, I placed the truck in park before nervously ripping the envelope open.

Dear Marisol,

First, I want to start off by saying that no matter what you think I love you and I'm sorry for my actions lately. If you're reading this letter, I have moved on to join Carlos. My guilt couldn't allow me to be around you with all that I know has happened. Let me just get to the point- Carlos and Lisa were

having an affair and Rich killed him because of it. He told me
this out his own mouth. This is the reason why I cut him off. He
threatened my life and I know it's a matter of time before he kills
me, so I just want to make things right. Please forgive me for
keeping this from you.
Love you forever,
Jade

I was in a complete state of shock and at this point I
don't know who to trust or what to believe.

Chapter 4

Lisa

Every time I looked in the mirror I was reminded of that bitch Denie. As I rubbed the permanent scar on my neck, thoughts of the day she held a knife firmly against my throat instantly pissed me off. I was also in disbelief that Denie had actually tried to poison me. I hated to admit it, but if Rich hadn't come into the room, she would've probably killed me. His cheating, trifling-ass had definitely saved my life, but to this day it was still hard for me to thank him for heroic actions. Every time I thought about how Marisol and Rich had an affair behind my back made me hate his ass even more than I already did. How could Marisol let me raise her child after all these years and then come back and claim her after I did all the hard work? Along with Rich and Denie, that bitch Marisol was also on my shit list. Or should I say…hit list? I had plans to get them all back one way or the other.

Now that I didn't have anyone else in my corner, anyone to love me, or anything to live for, I didn't give a fuck about anyone else's feelings. Burying my son was the hardest thing I'd ever done in my life, so I definitely had a 'fuck the world' attitude. Not to mention, I'm sure Marisol had something to do with his death, so I wanted to get her back first. Every time I thought about Juan's closed casket funeral it made me enraged. Apparently, the damage to his face was so bad, they wouldn't allow me to see him. What mother wouldn't wanna see their son one last time?

Her ass is gonna be sick once she finds out about me and Carlos, I thought.

My blood started to boil as I thought back to a few months ago and how my life had changed drastically. Not only was I upset with everybody else, but I was also pissed off at my fucking mother. She along with that no good ex-husband of mine had conspired with each other and gotten me committed into Saint Elizabeth's Mental Institution a month after Denie tried to take my life. How they'd come up with the conclusion that I was mentally disturbed was beyond me. I wasn't crazy and I was tired of people treating me like a damn charity case.

When I first arrived, I didn't trip about it as much because I was still mourning Juan's death and trying to get over my traumatic, near death experience, so my outbursts were a little out of control. On top of that, I was under the impression that I could sign myself out. However, after realizing that Rich, my mother or the doctor assigned to my case were the only ones able to sign my release papers, I became furious. The fact that Rich and my mother would play with my damn life like that had me enraged most of the time. Mental hospitals were made for sociopaths and schizophrenic motherfuckers who drooled all day. Not a distraught mother who'd just been through some tough times. I couldn't even consider myself crazy after killing Carlie. Sure, I'd taken an innocent child's life, but she was much better off being with my Heavenly Father than being raised by Rich.

Despite my ill feeling toward her, I'd been trying to be nice to my mother and prove to her that nothing was wrong with me, but obviously that shit wasn't working. I'd been in this fucking hell hole four months and it didn't seem like I was getting out anytime soon.

As thoughts continued to jump around in my head, I was finally interrupted by one of the nurses named, Betty. She was an older, black heavy-set woman with gray hair and massive breasts, who also had a sweet spirit. But no matter how nice she was to me, I just couldn't allow myself to be kind to anyone in this Godforsaken place.

"Well, hello Ms. Lisa. Why do you have it so dark in here? Let's get you some sun," Nurse Betty said, in a chipper mood as she opened the blinds.

"Who the hell wants to look out of a window that has bars?" I responded irritated as hell.

"Well, if you shed some light in this room it might make you feel better."

"Look, what do you want, lady?"

"It's time for you to take your meds and go visit with your psychiatrist."

It was at that moment, when I noticed the famous silver tray in her hand along with two cups.

"Y'all are gonna stop treating me like I'm crazy!" I snapped.

"Okay, Lisa let's have a good day today. Come on, open up and take your medicine," Nurse Betty said, as she handed me one cup that contained two pink pills and another cup filled with water.

After being in the hospital for several weeks, I finally learned that I was being given several anti depressant pills called Paxil. I hated taking the pills since they normally gave me terrible headaches and sometimes insomnia, but I still complied because I didn't want any trouble. If I was gonna get out of here, the most important thing to learn was self control.

Minutes later, Nurse Betty swapped her silver tray with a wheelchair and rolled it into my room.

"Is the chair really necessary?" I asked. "I do have two legs if you hadn't noticed."

"You should know by now that it's standard procedure,

Lisa," Nurse Betty replied.

I'm sure she thought I could be a complete bitch at times, but being an older nurse in this institution, I'm also sure she'd seen it all.

As Nurse Betty wheeled me to the psychiatrist's office, I was very uncomfortable watching the other patients. Eyeing most of their blank, delusional stares I had yet to get used to the atmosphere or the disgusting smell. Instead of a disinfected scent most hospitals were known for, this place had a sewage stench that made me want to throw up half the time. I couldn't believe my own mother thought it was best for me to be here. Patients were talking to themselves, screaming at their imaginary friends, and one lady was banging her head against the wall. It was imperative that I got out of this place quick before I became a product of my environment. Moments later, we finally we made it to the psychiatrist's office.

"Thanks for bringing Lisa down, Betty," Dr. Ju said. Once Betty nodded her head and walked away, the doctor turned to me. "Well, hello Lisa, how are you feeling today?"

She was a thin, very fashionable Asian woman who was in her early thirties. During every session, Dr. Ju irritated me because she always made me feel like I was less than her when I'm sure my closet would make her green with envy.

"How do you think I feel? I'm in this place as if I really need fucking help. I'm not like the rest of these people and you know it. Banging their heads and shit. I don't do that."

"I understand your frustration, Lisa, that's why I'm here to help you. I want you to get better so you can go home to your family. Trust me, I'm on your side."

"Well, get me out of here. My ex-husband and my mother committed me on purpose. They both hate me!"

"I want to help you get out, but over the course of four months, we still haven't made much progress. This is going to be a long road to recovery if you continue to shut me out. Can you at least give me a chance to help you?"

I rolled my eyes. "Whatever."

"Let's get started. So, during your last session we discussed your childhood and you seemed to be very fond of your dad. Then we spoke about the birth of your son, Juan, and the relationship you had with him. On your intake sheet that your mother filled out, it states you also have a daughter, where's your daughter now?"

"I don't have any children, and I would rather if we spoke about something else."

Dr. Ju wrote something down on a piece of paper before continuing. "Okay, well let's talk about your husband, Juan Sanchez Sr., he's known as Rich, correct?"

"Rich is my *ex*-husband. We've been divorced now for almost a year."

"Oh, sorry. So, was he was your first love?"

"Once upon a time I thought Rich was the best thing that ever happened to me. When we were young we were so happy. If he would've never been in that car accident, our lives would've probably been different."

"Why do you say that?" Dr. Ju inquired.

"Well, he was a basketball star in high school and there was talk of him being drafted right into the NBA. Well, all that changed when he was in a nearly fatal car accident."

"How so?"

"He started to get involved in the streets heavily and that's when the infidelity started, which ultimately made our lives a lot harder."

"Was he a good father to his children?"

"He was a great father to his daughter, but he hated my son."

"So, you said earlier that you didn't have any children and didn't wanna talk about it. Can I ask why?"

"Because I don't." I was aggravated all of a sudden.

"Lisa, you've gotta learn how to deal with problems if you ever want to get better," Dr. Ju advised. "You were doing so good. Don't shut down now."

I let out a huge sigh, then paused for a moment. *Maybe if*

I give this bitch want she wants she'll let me out of here, I thought. "Both my son and daughter passed away."

"I'm so sorry to hear that. How did they die?"

"My son was murdered and my daughter, well she…she's not here anymore."

"What happened to your daughter?" Dr. Ju questioned.

"Whatever they told you they lied!" I quickly yelled. At that moment, I got hyped. "I didn't mean to kill Carlie, but when Rich took his brother, Carlos away from me and I found out Carlos wasn't her father, I just couldn't help myself."

Dr. Ju looked at me strangly. "So, what did you do Lisa?"

"Rich did it. When he killed Carlos he messed everything up. It's his fault."

She wrote something down on her piece of paper once again. A part of me knew I shouldn't have told a stranger my business, but it felt good getting everything out.

"So, you're saying that Rich killed his brother?"

"Yes."

"What happened with your daughter?"

"I don't have a daughter! You're trying to trick me. I told you it's all Rich's fault. He cheated on me for years. He messed up my life. He was the reason why I started messing with Carlos in the first place!"

Ms. Ju could tell that I didn't want to talk about Carlie anymore, so she decided to keep the focus on Rich. We talked about his constant cheating for what seemed like hours, but when we got to the warehouse situation I froze. Anytime I went back to that place, it made me feel like I'd fallen inside of a dark hole. As I relived me getting raped, along with what I'd done to Denie in the same place, Denie walked in. I couldn't even finish telling Ms. Ju what happened.

"I know damn well you people ain't thinking about letting this looney bin bitch out of here. I came to let you know firsthand that she's crazy!" Denie yelled.

"Who the hell let you in here Denie?" I screamed, then

lunged at her. She wasn't about to mess up my chances for freedom.

As my fists made contact with each section of her face, I was determined to make her ass pay for trying to kill me. I owed her this beat down.

"Look at my neck! You did this shit to me," I shouted in a fit of rage.

"Lisa, stop!" Dr. Ju screamed as she shielded herself. "I'm not Denie!"

All of a sudden the office was filled with three male hospital orderlies dressed in all white uniforms. Moments later, another nurse came in and stuck something in my arm. I never had a chance to react before there was an instant cold rush in my veins and I passed out.

Chapter 5

Rich

In exactly two days, I'd managed to go through the entire twenty g's that I'd taken from Marisol. Not that it was hard, since it was short change to begin wit'. Even before Juan died my money was fucked up, but even more so after findin' out my son was an informant. I'd been chillin' tryin' to get off of the Feds radar, so goin' back to street narcotics wasn't an option at the momemt. Now, I had to think of other ways to get dough. Wit' Lisa in the crazy house, there was nothin' stoppin' me from breakin' into her house in order to work on my next plan. The answer to all my problems was in my old home, and there was nothin' anyone was goin' to do to stop me. Not even that nosey, worrisome-ass mother of hers.

Since Lisa's mother and I had admitted her into Saint Elizabeth a few months ago we had to keep contact, but it still didn't stop us from our constant bickerin'. The reason for me callin' my ex-mother-in-law once Lisa was damn near poisoned to death was to make sure Lisa had someone to take care of her. I knew Lisa's ass was gonna be unstable after that shit, so what better person to take on that problem than her own mother. But sometimes I wondered if it was a mistake involvin' her. The bitch seemed more interested in how much money Lisa got from me, and livin' in some shit that wasn't hers, then actually takin' care of her daughter.

As I drove down Military Road, the more upset I got. Just because I'd chosen the wrong bitch as my wife, all the money I'd spent over the years to live comfortably and enjoy life was now gone. My life was a mess. The thought of Lisa made my blood boil. When I got to the street I once called my own, suddenly I felt a rush.

Parkin' around back to go unnoticed, I thought of the best way to enter the house. Then it clicked, *the basement.* The bathroom window near the gym was the best place to go in un-detected and was the easiest to repair later. After scopin' out the house to make sure Lisa's mother wasn't there, I picked up a small brick, broke the window, and made my way inside.

This is some bullshit breakin' into my own fuckin' spot, I thought to myself.

Once I walked up the stairs of the basement, I passed the kitchen and made my way to the foyer. After smellin' the fresh scent of fried fish, it was obvious that Lisa's mother had defi-nitely moved in. At first I thought she might've been stayin' just to handle some of Lisa's business like bills and shit, but now it seemed like the bitch had a new address. If that was the case, I had to act fast.

Skippin' steps, I ran straight upstairs to the master bed-room. I needed a get rich quick plan and I knew Lisa held the cards. Before I made my way to the bedroom that would hope-fully be mine again, I stopped at Juan's room. Everything was still the same. Lisa and her mother hadn't even bothered to pick up his clothes from off the floor. I could still smell his scent, which surprisingly hurt me to the core. Although we didn't get along most of the time, I couldn't deny the fact that I missed my son. As I began to think about his laughter and flashy ways, my phone rang. I was instantly annoyed when the number popped up.

"Man, what do you want?" I snapped.

"I assume you're on your way to get your daughter."

"Trixie, don't keep callin' my phone. You gettin' on my fuckin' nerves. I told you I'm gonna pick her up. I'm takin' care of somethin' right now."

"Well, I have something to do and you said you would be here a couple of hours ago."

"Bitch, I don't have to explain myself to you. Just sit there and wait!" I yelled, then hung up.

Decidin' to turn off my phone, so Trixie couldn't disturb me anymore, I continued toward Lisa's bedroom. She didn't think too far these days, so I was sure that it wouldn't be long before I found the paperwork I needed. The first place I thought to look was her top lingerie drawer. She was known to keep odd and important items there in the past. When I opened the drawer, I didn't find the paperwork, but I did find a huge mandingo dildo.

"Freaky bitch," I said, shakin' my head at the long, fake dick.

Then I found her journal. At first I told myself to put it back since we were no longer married, but my curiosity quickly got the best of me. Flippin' through the pages, I read a few entries about how bad Lisa felt for what she'd done to Denie which was surprisin'. It was good to know that she felt completely responsible for her actions. Thinkin' there would be more entries, I continued to flip. However, what I found next, made me sick to my stomach. The shit written on the page could've sent me straight to jail.

Dear Carlos,

I'm sorry for what has happened between us. You have to forgive me. I will never forgive Rich for taking your life. He did this to us, so I really hope you don't blame me. I love you and the only reason I've gone along with his plan is because he threatened to kill me, too. My son and our unborn child needed me. I promise you I'll make him pay one day. I promise you that.

Until tomorrow, Love you much.
Lisa

There were pages and pages of letters like that written to Los. The more I read, I realized that committin' Lisa's ass had definitely been the right choice. She was unstable, and needed to be put away for everyone's own good.

Rememberin' I had a job to do, the next place I looked was under the mattress. Pushin' the king sized pillowtop up in the air, I immediately spotted a manila envelope. Thinkin' it was exactly what I was lookin' for, I grabbed the envelope before sittin' the mattress back down. After takin' a quick peek inside, I pulled everything out and sifted through the papers. Juan's social security card, death certificate, even his old high school transcripts were all there. The envelope also included old bank statements, the deed to my old bar, Bottom's Up and several other important items. Why she kept all those things under the bed and not in our home office, was beyond me. I was startin' to think that I had to look somewhere else, until I glanced at the last piece of paper. Bam, there it was...three life insurance documents. As I scanned one of the documents, a huge smile suddenly appeared on my face. This had turned into my lucky day because there it was in black and white. I was the beneficiary of a $750,000 policy if somethin' ever happened to Lisa. The dumb bitch had obviously never bothered to change anything when we got divorced.

Grabbin' the paperwork, I folded all the sheets in half then stuffed them into my back pocket. After placin' the envelope back, I was just about to walk out of the bedroom door before noticin' Lisa's white Chanel ceramic watch with custom diamonds on the dresser. I'd paid a good ten stacks for that watch and I figured Lisa didn't have a need for it now anyway.

I could get a good eight thousand for this shit, I thought to myself.

No sooner than I put it in my pocket, I then noticed a credit card on dresser as well. After lookin' at the name, Doris L. Carter, I realized that it belonged to Lisa's mother. Decidin' to teach that bitch a lesson for stayin' where she didn't belong, I slipped that shit in my pocket, too.

Makin' my way down the steps, I quickly jumped when I saw someone walkin' in the front door. It was Lisa's mother. We both scared the shit out of each other.

She immediately clenched her chest. "Rich, what in the world are you doing here? You almost gave me a heart attack!"

All of her groceries had fallen out of the bag and onto the floor of the foyer, broken eggs and all.

"What up, First Lady?" I stepped over the bag and walked toward the family room.

"You rude-ass bastard! Didn't your mother teach you any manners? How the hell are you just gonna walk over the bag instead of helping me pick this stuff up. It's your fault it fell in the first place."

"Wow, is that the way a lady of the cloth is supposed to speak? Now, what would your husband have to say about that mouth of yours? Besides, you straight. It looks like you could do some more bends and reaches to help your mid area anyway." I patted my stomach and smiled.

She gave me a look of death. "Don't go there. If my husband was alive, you wouldn't be here talking trash. Now, answer my question, why are you here? You don't live here anymore. How the hell did you get in anyway? The locks were changed."

"I have my ways. Besides, maybe I should be askin' you the same question since your ass don't live here either This isn't your house."

"Well, this is my daughter's house, so I have a right to stay here as long as I want."

"The entire time me and my family lived here, you never stepped foot in this damn house, so you should've kept it that way, First Lady."

"That's not my damn name. I'm Mrs. Carter to you."

"If I were you, I wouldn't get too comfortable. What…do you think some other money hungry Pastor muthafucka gon' be livin' up in here with you? I don't think so. It'll only be a matter of time before this place is mine again."

"Over my dead body!"

"Now you know that can be arranged."

She stared at me for what seemed like forever before breakin' out into a prayer. "Father God, please keep me near the cross before I hurt this man. He's the devil, the devil I tell you!" she shouted with her hands in the air.

Luckily, before she could start some sort of fake-ass sermon, the house phone rang. With the egg carton in her hand, she quickly turned around and walked into the kitchen. Mrs. Carter's swagger had definitely changed since her husband passed away. I'd rarely been around her over the years, but every time I saw her she always looked like a preacher's wife, church hat and all. Lately she'd been a different person, or maybe this is who she was all along. Her once gray hair was now red and cut into a short, Halle Berry spiky style and it looked as if her golden colored skin had a recent dose of Botox. Even her thick eyebrows had now been arched. If she wasn't pushin' sixty-five I would blame it on a mid life crisis. Maybe Lisa was just like her mother, a sheep in wolf's clothin'.

Since I'd found what I was lookin' for anyway, there was no need for me to argue wit' the witch any longer. Just as I started out the door, the bitch called my name.

"Rich, oh my goodness, that was the hospital. Lisa had a session with her doctor the other day and attacked her. Apparently Lisa also said some things that have them concerned."

"And please tell me why I should give a fuck. Lisa is always sayin' crazy shit. What else is new?"

"First of all you need to show some respect. Last time I checked, this is something we both signed up for. Furthermore, her doctor is requesting to speak with you about the session."

"Man, I'm not tryin' to talk to no doctor about Lisa hittin' her. They should be able to handle that. I got better shit to do. Lisa ain't my problem no more."

"I think it's more than that. Whatever my poor child has told them, the doctor seems to only wanna discuss it with you."

She handed me a piece of paper that had a phone number on it. "That's the doctor's direct line."

Now, I was concerned. "Aight, I'll call her."

"Lord Jesus, I need to go up to the hospital right now to see what's going on. If something happens to my daughter, her blood is on your hands!"

"My hands. You just said we signed up for this shit together!"

"We did, but that doesn't mean I trust you. Obviously, something isn't right."

"Whatever!"

As I walked out of the door actin' as if I wasn't phased, my heart was literally in my stomach. Just in case Lisa had said somethin' to incriminate me, I needed to check into that patient confidentiality thing ASAP. My best bet was to call the hospital as soon as I got in the car so that Mrs. Carter didn't try to pry. After jumpin' inside, I quickly pulled out my phone, turned it on, then dialed the number from the piece of paper. Nervously waitin' for someone to answer, the phone rung at least four times before Dr. Ju's voicemail came on. I left her a message and decided to wait for her to call me back instead of just goin' up there. It was no tellin' what Lisa had said, so I wanted to make sure I wasn't walkin' into a set-up. For all I knew, the fuckin' cop could've been waitin' on me when I got there. Still feelin' a little nervous, I pulled out the driveway before headin' toward Trixie's house since that bitch had already started blowin' my phone up again.

Chapter 6

Rich

"I know damn well this bitch don't think I'm fuckin' her," I mumbled to myself as I approached Trixie's door.

Standin' in the doorway wit' a revealin' red negligee on, she looked just like a broke-ass Victoria Secret model. As a matter of fact, the lingerie was one of the pieces I'd bought her from La Perla back in the day. Maybe her triflin'-ass thought puttin' on somethin' sexy would get some sparks flyin' between us. Even though her body looked phat to death as usual, pussy was the furthest from my mind. Little did she know every time I pulled up to her house, I instantly got pissed off when flashbacks to me killin' that nigga Mike in the same spot entered my mind. The thought of that dude raisin' my daughter, Juanita all this time made my blood boil, so fuckin' was the last thing on my mind.

I looked at Trixie up and down. I hated that she'd dyed her hair back blonde and cut it short. Even though it looked so much better jet black, the style did make her high cheek bones stand out.

"So, is this the reason you been blowin' my phone up?

Where's my daughter?" I asked, walkin' in the door.

"Rich please, I don't want your ass. The only thing that's going on between us is Juanita."

"Bitch whatever! You know damn well you ain't never turned down this good dick," I replied with a smirk.

"Lower your voice with all that dumb shit, asshole. I have company."

Once I made my way to the livin' room, some young dude was sittin' on the couch wit' a wife beater and his shoes off lookin' like he'd made himself right at home. To make matters worse, he had a blunt in his hand and looked high as hell. There was no way I could hold back.

"You fuckin' whore! So, you laid up wit' some nigga in front of my damn daughter? Smokin' weed and shit! What the hell kind of mother are you? That muthafucka looks half your age!"

Trixie placed her hands on her small waist. "Don't come up in here judging me. Besides, if your ass would'a been on time Juanita wouldn't be here, now would she?"

"Who the fuck is this nigga?" I shot back muggin' on the dude.

"None of your damn business!" Trixie retaliated.

"Look, man I ain't here tryna cause no drama. Me and Trixie just met the other day. I mean Trix you cool and all, but I ain't tryna come between nuffin'," the dude said, actin' like a real punk.

"He's just my daughter's father. I don't fuck with him like that," Trixie tried to explain.

"No, bitch don't try and twist the shit up. I don't fuck wit' you like that," I shot back. "Does this nigga know what kind of connivin' bitch you are?"

Just when I was ready to go in on Trixie again, my daughter ran up to me at full speed.

"Daddy! Daddy!" Juanita screamed full of smiles.

"Hey, baby girl. How are you?" I quickly scooped her up in my arms.

"I'm fine. I missed you, Daddy."

"I missed you, too, baby," I said, givin' her a kiss on her forehead. "You ready to go? Where's your bag?" When Juanita shrugged her shoulders, I turned back toward Trixie who looked as if she was pleadin' wit' the grade school nigga not to go. "Where's Juanita's stuff?"

"In her room. If you wanna take her somewhere, then you pack the damn bag," Trixie replied in a nasty tone.

Bitin' my bottom lip, I wanted to walk up on that bitch and slap the shit out of her ass for disrespectin' me, but didn't want Juanita to see me do that to her mother. If I wanted her to grow up to be a strong, black woman and not take shit from a man, I had to lead by example. For once, I had to take the high road.

At that moment, I walked Juanita upstairs to her room so we could get her stuff together. One good thing I could say about Trixie was that she kept my daughter fly as hell. Her closet was full of Flowers by Zoe, Juicy, and True Religions. She always looked cute…real girly, which I liked. Juanita talked me to death as I packed her bag. Daddy this and Daddy that, is what she constantly said, which made me smile every time she called me that. Over the past few months, I really enjoyed spendin' time wit' my baby girl, and hoped she felt the same. I was really tryin' to be a better father. The last thing I wanted was for our relationship to end up like me and Denie or even me and Juan. I'd obviously failed wit' both of them somewhere down the line, and didn't want the same thing to happen again.

"Daddy, it's lighting up," Juanita said, then pointed to the green light illuminatin' from the top of my phone.

After takin' it out of the holster, I looked at the caller-ID. I immediately recognized the 202 number. It was the hospital.

"Hello," I answered in my best professional voice.

"Yes, may I please speak with Mr. Juan Sanchez?"

"Speakin'. How can I help you?"

"Hello, this is Dr. Ju calling from Saint Elizabeth's how are you today?"

"I'm blessed." I had to hold back a chuckle from the way I was talkin'. "Mrs. Carter told me to contact you because there was some concern about my ex-wife."

"Yes. During our session a few days ago Lisa had what we call a relapse. She attacked me thinking I was your daughter, Denie. We had to sedate her, but she seems to be in a better place now. I apologize for taking so long to inform you and Mrs. Carter. I took some time off after the incident and this is my first day back."

"Really. Well, I'm so sorry about that, Dr. Ju."

"There's no need to apologize for Lisa's actions. I'm actually quite used to irate patients. My concern however lies with what she revealed during our session. Now, normally there is a patient confidentiality policy that we adhere to, but it appears as if Lisa didn't sign the proper paperwork when she first arrived. In that case we are allowed to inform spouses about patient sessions."

I continued to listen and hoped that Dr. Ju would hurry up and get to the point.

"Mr. Sanchez, I do realize that you and Lisa are no longer married, which technically doesn't make you her spouse, but since you were the one who sought help for Lisa in the first place, I'm making an exception."

"Great. So, what is this all about?"

"There was an incident that took place in a warehouse that she spoke of. Now, I was a bit confused, let me look at my notes here." I could hear Dr. Ju shufflin' some papers. "She spoke about Denie trying to kill her for what happened in the warehouse. Do you know anything about this?"

"Dr. Ju, my ex-wife is really sick and I don't understand why she would say such a thing."

"She also revealed in the session that you murdered your brother, Carlos because they had an affair and how much she missed him."

My eyes increased. *Wait a minute. What the fuck did that bitch just say*, I thought. "Excuse me?"

"Your wife told me that you killed your brother, Carlos, Mr. Sanchez," she repeated.

I was speechless. I couldn't believe Lisa had been runnin' her fuckin' mouth. I didn't care if she was doin' it as part of her treatment or not. Talkin' reckless was unacceptable at any time.

"Mr. Sanchez, are you there?" Dr. Ju asked.

"I'm here. Umm…yes, my brother was murdered last year." I had to get my thoughts together and fast.

"Daddy…you ready to…" Juanita said, right before I quietly told her to be quiet.

"It really saddens me that my wife is this sick, and makes up these delusional stories," I carried on.

"So, you're saying that all the things she's been disclosing are false?"

"Oh, most definitely." I wanted to say, 'bitch why would you believe one of your crazy-fuckin' patients anyway?'

"Well, that's makes me feel a lot better. I know the patients here can make false statements sometimes, and in this case I just wanted to be sure. Let me tell you this though Mr. Sanchez. Another reason why Lisa probably can't come out of this deep depression is because she's holding onto a great deal of remorse. She kept asking God to forgive her for killing the baby. She kept asking God, why he made you the father."

There was complete silence. I couldn't believe that Lisa had finally admitted to takin' my innocent baby girl's life.

"My daughter supposedly died of SIDS. Lisa, however, was the last person wit' her before she died, so I had a feelin' she was responsible."

"Well, Lisa's condition isn't getting any better, it's actually getting worse, especially her hallucinations. I'm thinking that we might need to do a hypnotic therapy treatment to see if we can get to the core of the problem. I might even ask you and her mother to be present, just in case there's something that's revealed from her childhood. The next time you come to the hospital I'll need both you and Mrs. Carter to sign off on consent."

"Oh, you can give her whatever treatment you want, I don't care. I'll sign whatever you want."

Dr. Ju was quiet for a minute. I guess she was surprised by my statement.

"Umm, okay."

"Thanks again for your call."

"I'll be in touch. Enjoy the remainder of your day."

"You too."

Holdin' back my anger in front of Juanita had proven to be a difficult task as the thought of Lisa tellin' her doctor about Carlos and admittin' to Carlie's death. I was so pissed off, I could've snapped that bitch's neck in two. For me that was all I needed to hear, Lisa really did have to go now. Until I could plan her demise I had to do damage control so she wouldn't run her mouth anymore. My plans wit' Juanita changed right away.

Makin' my way back downstairs, I wanted to let Trixie know that I would have to get Juanita later. But by the time Juanita and I made it to the livin' room, Trixie had the dude straddled and was fuckin' him like a true jockey. My anger toward Lisa combined by my daughter witnessin' her mother havin' sex immediately took me out of my body. Before Trixie could get up, I pulled her off of his dick, then punched the young guy straight in his face.

"Nigga, I can't believe you sittin' here fuckin' this whore while me and my daughter were upstairs." Enraged, I grabbed my gun from my waist and placed it against his head. "I can see you don't have no respect. Do you know who you fuckin' wit'?"

"Rich, no!" Trixie screamed.

Juanita screamed right along with her.

As I watched my baby girl wail, I slowly lowered the gun. It was this muthafucka's lucky day.

"Get the fuck out of here, you bitch-ass nigga," I ordered. I made sure to keep the gun in my hand just in case this clown felt brave.

Holdin' his face, the dude didn't hesitant grabbin' his clothes and runnin' out the door wit' just his tank top on. Puttin' my gun away, I walked over and punched Trixie in her face, too.

So much for my daughter seein' me in a positive light, I thought.

"You disrespectful bitch!"

"Rich, stop!" Trixie screamed. She held her hands up to protect herself.

"Don't ever let me catch you doin' that shit in front of my daughter again!"

"You fucked my money up!" she roared.

"Bitch, are you that pressed for a dollar?"

"I got bills! Your broke-ass ain't doing shit for us!"

When I looked at Trixie's face, I could tell she was gonna have a black eye.

"So, you think you're that bitch because you got an upgrade off my doe. Bitch, the money that bought you all this shit was mine. That bitch-ass nigga Mike you was fuckin' stole from me, remember?"

Trixie held onto her face. "Get out!"

"Daddy, no!" Juanita was in tears holdin' onto my leg.

"I'm sorry, baby. Mommy was being really bad. I'm sorry you had to see this." I kissed her forehead and started out the door.

Trixie yelled all kinds of obscenities as I headed toward my car. As bad as I wanted to go back and black her other eye I had business to take care of wit' Lisa at the hospital before that bitch got me caught up.

Chapter 7

Lisa

It was the first day I'd felt back to normal in the past twenty-four hours. Apparently after being pumped with tons of medication, the groggy feeling had finally subsided, but I still felt drained. From what Nurse Betty informed me, Dr. Ju was going around telling everyone that I'd attacked her during our last session. If that bitch was telling the truth, I damn sure didn't remember. All I know is that Becky's crazy-ass from down the hall kept telling me, 'congratulations' all day, so something must've happened. I honestly didn't remember. I just knew that I wanted my life back.

"Come on sweetie open up, you gotta get some food in your system. You're all skin and bones."

As my mother gathered a spoon full of mashed potatoes, I knocked that shit right out of her hand. I was so tired of her pity.

"Stop treating me like I'm five years old!" I yelled. "I don't want anything to eat!"

This time she grabbed the fork and stabbed some cold-ass string beans. "Come on, Lisa. The doctor said you haven't been eating well."

I held up my hand. "Don't bring that nasty food near me. I just told you that I don't want any."

"Why do you have to be so difficult," she said, putting the fork down. I could care less if her ass was frustrated.

"Because I'm in here that's why!" I yelled, sitting up in the bed. "Why don't you just get the hell out?"

"Look, Lisa I'm trying to help you get what's left of your life back on track. Don't be disrespectful to me. I've been praying to God that he helps you through this situation."

I stared at the small mole on my mother's left cheek. "Praying to God, really Ma? You never gave a damn about me, so don't try to act like you care now!"

She seemed hurt by my comment. "You're my daughter Lisa, I do care about you. How dare you say that?"

"Why now Ma, huh? Why now?"

"Did you forget that you're the one who shut your family out because of Rich? We never turned our backs on you, Lisa. You were always welcomed to come back home at anytime. You made the choice to be with Rich. Your mental state is because of him, so don't blame me."

"If Daddy was here, he wouldn't have committed me into this God forsaken place. This is your way of getting rid of me. I wouldn't be surprised if your money hungry-ass wasn't trying to take over my money."

"Money hungry? Are you serious, Lisa? I don't need anything from you, including your disrespect," my mother said as she got up. It looked like she was about to leave.

"You think I'm crazy, but I know more than you give me credit for. Just like you think I don't know my daddy had a will. He told me years ago that he was leaving me enough to get away from Rich and now all of a sudden there's no will. You think you're slick, but I know the real you. I know who the real Mrs. Carter is, underneath the big church hat."

"I told you your father didn't have a will dammit! That's all you care about Lisa is the money! Is this what Rich turned you into?"

"Last time I checked I wasn't stealing from the church behind Daddy's back. He told me a lot of things about you. I know that my brother, Brent, isn't Daddy's child. Yeah, all these years Junior really wasn't a junior. But you're supposed to be so much better than me. You've always been so quick to judge me and you're no different."

She stared at me for a few seconds. "Last time *I checked* I wasn't the one in a mental hospital, so at the end of the day Lisa, we're not that much alike. Have a nice life. Let your dead beat ex-husband care for you." She turned around. "Oh, speaking of the devil, Rich she's all yours."

My mother stormed out with angry tears, as Rich entered with a look in his eyes that I feared in the past. But today there was a new Lisa in town. I was ready for whatever his ass was serving.

Lately Rich had been looking back to his old self. For a minute it looked as if he'd fallen off, but today he'd cleaned up nice. The crisp grey Prada shirt he had on looked brand new. I wondered if he'd come into some money. I wondered if he was out flossing while I was wasting my time in a mental institution.

"And what can I help you with sir?" I asked sarcastically.

"Lisa, I don't have time to play games wit' you. What the fuck did you tell that doctor?"

I just had to snicker. "So, Rich the gangsta is here to off me. What the fuck do you mean what did I tell her?"

"Dr. Ju called questionin' me about the warehouse and Los. What the fuck did you tell them people?"

"Mr. Sanchez, I didn't ask to be here, remember? You and that fucked up ass mother of mine admitted me without my consent. If you hadn't brought me here you wouldn't have to worry about what I tell people now would you?"

"I'm so sick of your damn mouth."

"I don't care what you're sick of. If you don't get me out of here I just might keep running my mouth!"

Rich peeked his head out my room door before closing it.

He then walked over to me, wrapped my hair around his hand to make sure he had a good grip, then yanked my head to the side. He was obviously getting tired of my sarcasm, but I thought it was funny how pissed off he was.

"Listen bitch, I'm gonna ask you one more time what the fuck you told that doctor about me. She seems to think that I killed Los, but more than that she told me that you admitted to killin' Carlie."

My heart dropped to the pit of my stomach. There was no way Dr. Ju would've known about Carlie, so I really must've been talking too much. I hated that I couldn't remember exactly what I said. Me hackling Rich was no longer funny. The look in his eyes told me that he was ready for war and that it was only a matter of time before he would send me to my creator. Nobody fucked with a snitch. Even more than that, if he really knew that I'd killed the baby, I would definitely never make it out of this hospital alive. Suddenly, I was nervous about what I'd revealed.

"I didn't tell her anything like that!" I yelled in defense mode. "You're tripping."

"Well, how the fuck does she know about the ware-house? If you told her all that, then why shouldn't I believe that you killed my daughter?"

"You and Dr. Ju are making shit up. Why would I kill my own daughter? Carlie died of SIDS. And why would I incriminate myself by telling her about Carlos?"

"Bitch, because you're crazy, that's why."

"I'm not crazy! Stop saying that!"

If I had a knife I would've stabbed his ass right in this chest for calling me that.

"How does she know about the warehouse?" Rich repeated.

"I don't know, they…they drugged me up."

"So, you're admittin' it?"

I shook my head back and forth. "No, I didn't say that."

At that moment, Rich let go of my hair, but grabbed one of the pillows from behind me and attempted to place it over my face. If it wasn't for the terrifying scream I let out, he probably would've suffocated me without a second thought.

"Get the hell out of my room. You need to be in here, not me!" I belted.

"You're gonna pay for killin' my daughter and runnin' your fuckin' mouth."

"So, now you're threatening me."

"No, that's a promise. I've given you way too many passes. You should've paid for what you did to Denie a long time ago," Rich stated. "Consider yourself lucky to be breathin' right now."

All of a sudden my fear turned into bravery. "Rich, tell me what the fuck I have to live for anyway? If you kill me, who's gonna come to my funeral. Nigga, just do what you gotta do."

Just before he was about to respond, Dr. Ju walked in.

"Oh, hello Mr. Sanchez. Mrs. Carter stopped by before she left to let me know that you were here. I didn't know you were coming so soon. Are you ready to sign those papers?"

Rich quickly dropped the pillow. "I sure am."

"Wait, what papers? He's not even my husband anymore. He shouldn't even be talking to you!" I yelled.

"Dr. Ju, do you think I could ever sign Lisa out on a day pass or somethin'? Her birthday is comin' up, so I wanna celebrate like we used to," Rich said.

I hoped Dr. Ju could see the devious smile plastered across his face.

"He's lying. He just wants me out of here so he can kill me!" I roared.

"Lisa, please. Stop makin' up lies. Dr. Ju is on to you by now," Rich spoke as he ushered Dr. Ju out of the room.

As soon as they left, I knew I was on borrowed time now. There was no way Rich was gonna believe me now. It was a matter of time before he sent me to heaven with my son.

Chapter 8

Marisol

I made my way to the wine cellar and grabbed me something nice to calm my nerves. Normally, my dining room was only used for special occasions, but if things went as I hoped they would, this was certainly gonna be a night to remember. Popping open a bottle of white wine called *Freaky Muscato*, that my St. Louis partner sent me, I played with my mother of pearl .380 pistol I'd named, Miss Pearlie.

It had been days since Javier had given me the letter, and after walking around the house like a complete zombie, I was finally ready to confront Rich about the allegations of Carlos' death. Admiring the gun, I thought of how Rich had obviously betrayed me. It was still hard to believe that he was responsible for killing my husband. I'd been sleeping with the devil the entire time, and never had a clue. As I mourned Carlos' death and dealt with Mia being sick, Rich was there every step of the way. Now, I wondered if it was out of guilt, or if was he trying to keep close tabs on me for some reason. Obviously, I didn't really know who he was, so anything was possible at this point.

He'd crossed me, and I felt stupid now for loving him.

Realizing that the kids didn't need to be around, it was good that Denie was hanging out as usual and Maria had taken the girls to visit her sister in Alexandria. This was the perfect time for me to get to the bottom of all this, even if it meant me taking Rich's life.

"So, what's it gonna be Miss Pearlie, are you ready to put in some work?" I asked, then admired the beautiful cream handle.

Sipping my glass of wine, I was nice and relaxed. Even though I didn't do well with alcohol, I still had a clear mind. I was focused and tried my best to control my feelings. Moments later, my Blackberry buzzed against the table. It was Rich.

"Yeah," I tried my best to disguise my anger.

"You changed the gate code."

"I sure did. I'll buzz you in."

"Yeah, alright," he replied in a sarcastic tone.

Those days were over where he could come and go as he pleased in my home. I knew that move had fucked his head up, but he had no idea what was about to come next. I took a deep breath to try and get myself together. Taking my glass of wine to the head, I poured myself a second one, then downed that one as well. The shit definitely had me a little buzzed.

Maybe it'll help me get through the night sane, I thought.

Unlocking the door, I went back into the dining room and sat at the table.

"Marisol, where you at?" Rich yelled.

"I'm in the dining room!"

As soon as he walked inside, I had the gun aimed right at his chest.

Rich quickly raised both arms in the air. "What the fuck is this shit about?" He seemed surprised and cautious, not knowing whether to take me serious or not.

"You think I'm a joke, nigga. Have a seat. We have a lot to talk about."

When Rich saw tears streaming down my face, he knew I

meant business and complied.

"How could you, Rich? I trusted you."

"Man Trix...I mean Marisol, why the fuck you pointin' that gun at me? Now, I gotta come in your crib strapped? Why the fuck you trippin'?"

"For starters, you should get a bullet for calling me that bitch's name, and don't try to play dumb because I heard you. Your secret has been exposed muthafucka!" I threw Jade's letter at him.

As he scanned the paper, Rich shook his head in disbelief.

"Are you ready to come clean?" I questioned. Standing up, I walked over to him and this time placed the gun to this temple.

"As a matter of fact I am. I'm tired of holdin' this shit in. Yes, I'm ready to tell you everything."

"Speak, you fucking traitor!"

It looked like he wanted to fire off some type of sarcastic-ass response, but knew that would've been a dumb move.

"It all started one night I saw Lisa out Baltimore while I was handlin' some business. I wondered what the fuck she was doin' out there, so I followed her. She ended up at some rundown hotel. I didn't know what type of shit that bitch was involved in because around that time her attitude had changed. So..."

I pushed the gun further into the side of his head. "What the hell does this have to do with my husband?"

"Marisol, I'm gettin' to that just calm down," Rich responded. "Anyway, so I gave it a minute and figured that I would let Lisa get comfortable before I barged in the room to see what was up. Once I broke the door down, it was dark and I started bussin' off. Once I turned the light on, the first thing I saw was Lisa naked in the bed screamin'. Man, my mind went crazy. I was so fuckin' pissed that I wasn't even focused on who she was in there wit'. Next thing I know, I had a gun to my head. Once he spoke, I couldn't believe it was Los. I also couldn't believe how the nigga had the audacity to tell me that he loved her. He went on and on about how I didn't deserve Lisa because I didn't know how to treat a real woman."

"So, let me get this straight, my husband actually told you he loved Lisa?"

"Yeah."

I smiled. "Is that the best you can do Rich? You know what, my patience is wearing thin, so please give me a reason not to fucking kill you right now!"

"Marisol, just listen to me!" he yelled as his eyes suddenly watered.

In all the years I'd known Rich, there was only one time I'd ever seen him cry, and that was when his mother died. He instantly got my attention once I saw some type of emotion.

"All I could think about was how me and you had slept together back in the day and maybe God was punishin' me. I was hurt."

"So, you killed him because of that bitch?"

"No, I didn't kill him. I jumped on him and tried to beat the shit out of him, since I didn't think he would shoot me. We were fightin' like two dudes who didn't even know each other when my gun fell. Next thing I knew Lisa was screamin', tellin' us to stop or she would shoot. She pointed my gun and everything, but we still didn't stop. That's when the gun went off a few times. At first I thought I was hit, but she'd missed me and hit Los. I didn't know what to do at that point. The nigga I loved more than anything was dead in my arms. Lisa killed my brother, Marisol. Now you know why I hate her so much."

To say that I was in shock would've been an understatement. I couldn't believe what I was hearing. My husband who I loved and mourned had been fucking Lisa right up under my nose. My heart ached, and I didn't know how to react to this news. Sitting back down, I placed the gun on the table before running my hands down my face. This shit was a devastating blow.

"So, Rich tell me, how did Carlos end up in The Chesapeake Bay left to die?"

"He was already dead. I panicked and figured that I had to protect my kids. I didn't give a fuck about Lisa, but I knew that if Uncle Renzo found out what happened, not only would he kill Lisa, he would take Denie and Juan's lives as well. I covered up his murder to protect my kids. I know that I kept this from you, but I just didn't know how to tell you. I wondered if you would expose the truth to Renzo."

For some reason the soft spot I had for Rich was my weakness. As crazy as it seemed, I actually believed him. What was I to do now? My mind was all over the place and I needed more answers.

"So, what did Jade have to do with this and why would she say you killed Carlos?"

"That night I had a room and Jade was waitin' for me. I was distraught once I got there and told her what happened. She was upset that I followed Lisa to begin wit'. She made it more about me and Lisa than her really understandin' the bigger fuckin' picture. She was always threatened by Lisa, and when I catch that bitch she's gonna pay for this shit!"

"Well, just in case you didn't know, Jade is dead, and her family thinks that you're responsible."

"What? Who told you that shit?" he asked with an alarming expression.

"Her brother Javier. Jade can actually rot in hell for all I care. No friend of mine that I treated like family would keep something from me and protect a dude she just met. Did you threaten her or something?"

"No. I was gonna tell you everything, but Jade felt it was best that you didn't know. She's the one who felt that you would go straight to Renzo wit' this."

"What?" I yelled.

"I mean you can't fault her. Carlos was your husband," Rich replied.

"Yeah, he was, but that bitch didn't know what the fuck I would've done."

"I feel ya. We had a big fall out over all this. Jade told me since I was so concerned about Lisa she never wanted to see me again."

If Rich was lying about all this, he deserved a damn Oscar. Something deep inside was telling me to proceed with caution, but my heart was telling me that Rich would never intentionally hurt his own brother. I always felt that Carlos and Rich loved each other more than they loved me or Lisa, so maybe he was telling the truth.

"You all betrayed me. You, Carlos, Jade, and Lisa ain't shit. Why didn't you just tell me, Rich? I thought we were better than that. Now, I don't know what or who to believe. This is just all too much to deal with, just get out!"

"I'm not leavin' you like this," he said, making his way closer to me. "I love you, Marisol. If I didn't love you, I would've never forgiven you for what you did to Denie. I mean you left my newborn daughter on my fuckin' doorstep. She's fucked up wit' me because of all this, and here I am still lovin' you."

He knew how to get to me. No matter what, a part of me felt like I owed both him and Denie. As Rich reached out to hold me, I immediately felt vulnerable. I didn't know if it was the wine or my emotional overload, but I let him hold me. Strangely, I felt safe.

"Marisol, I'm sorry for hurtin' you. We actually hurt each other. Let's try and move on and focus on raisin' Denie to be better than us. Everything happens for a reason. Maybe this is our second chance to be together and do what's right. There are other things that take precedence, Mia's condition for starters, and the business. Lisa is going to pay. Trust me, I have a plan for that bitch. You let me handle that. Her doctor told me that she admitted to killing Carlie."

Let's see who gets to her first, I thought to myself. She was gonna pay for killing Carlos, too.

As Rich tried to slide his hand down to the small of my back, I knew what he was up to. However, I didn't fight it because I was definitely in need of some sex, even if it came from Rich. We hadn't slept together in months, so I'd been on a serious sex drought lately. Rich was my comfort zone and that's why I allowed him to carry me upstairs to my bedroom.

"I love you girl," Rich whispered as he laid me down on my bed and began kissing me on my stomach.

His tongue played with my navel before he took off my leggings, made his way down to my vajayjay and started flickering his tongue against my clit. His warm mouth felt so good as he took his fingers to spread my lips apart. Once Rich got further inside, he went right to work. Making love to my pussy with his mouth, he soon started taking off his pants. Never to be outdone in the bedroom, it wasn't long before I maneuvered my way to his dick and took him whole. Yeah, deep throat was my specialty. But that wasn't the end because that wine had me feeling quite frisky. I was ready to get my freak on. After jumping on top of him, I quickly inserted his tool, then took it like a true stallion.

"Tell me this is the best pussy you ever had," I demanded.

"Why you think I keep comin' back? I love this shit."

Riding his dick to the perfect rhythm, Rich placed his hands along my waist as I slid my dripping pussy down his pole. He then buried his face in my breasts as I suddenly sped up the tempo. He never could really handle me on top and sex with him always felt like a competition of, who was gonna defeat who. I could feel his penis jerk as he tried to hold back from cumming, then quickly pulled out.

"I ain't ready for this shit to end," Rich said in a low tone.

Flipping me onto my stomach, he entered my nest from behind, fucking me fast…and hard.

"Tell me you love this dick!" he yelled, then smacked my ass.

"I love it Rich, ahhhh, I love it."

His rock hard dick banged against my walls with so

much force, I thought my head was gonna go through the head-board. As his body began to shake, I played with my pussy to make sure my climax was even more explosive. Within seconds, my thighs began to vibrate and a tingling sensation raced down my back. We both came at the same time.

As soon as Rich collapsed on top of me, he gave my right cheek two soft, delicate kisses.

"Did you missed me, babe?"

"Yeah, I did."

No matter how much I let Rich fuck me, he would never get another chance to fuck me over. I had to come up with a plan to make sure what he told me was true. As I laid in bed with moistness between my legs, I thought about how Lisa was gonna pay for what she'd done.

And so is Rich, if he's lying.

Chapter 9

Denie

Damn, what a night I thought to myself as I crept in the house through my back entrance.

I didn't feel like the interrogation on where I'd been all night, especially since it was two in the afternoon. But thinking back on it, Chanel and I had a damn blast. I'd met Chanel a few months ago while going to see Nelson in prison down in Petersburg, VA. Her boyfriend, Stan, was locked up at the same time, so we instantly connected and had been road dogs ever since. Even though I'd made it clear to Nelson that, 'I didn't do prison' well and had no intentions of fucking with him while he was locked up, at least I'd met a true friend.

She was always down for whatever. After hitting up the Wizards vs. Celtics playoff game, we went straight to the after party at Bar 7. Since I was still on my 'revenge against Lisa' mode, I thought it was the right moment to make my move on Cornell Willis. I knew that she was already at the edge of the cliff, and this was my plan to push that bitch all the way off. These athletes were such marks, so I knew it wasn't gonna be a problem baiting him. He was so easy to get it kinda pissed me off. I was ready for a huge challenge, but I guess I was just that good. By the end of the night, he'd hit me off with courtside seats to the next game. I guess he thought that was his way of trying to get in my pants, but little did he know, I loved to fuck. It wasn't about his money. I had my own. It was about getting in his head. I didn't have love for none of these niggas out here.

As I laid across my bed, I laughed at the text messages coming in from Cornell.

Did you make it home yet? I told you to hit me to let me know

Yeah I'm home, I texted him back.

Cool, baby I had a good time last night. Can we do dinner later on?

How does Morton's Steakhouse sound?

Sounds good to me, Naomi how about 7, he wrote

Bet, I replied.

I went by my middle name, Naomi, so he wouldn't know that I had any connection to Lisa. People were always talking about how cheap that nigga Cornell was, but he hadn't even got the pussy yet, and I was already on his mind.

I guess I'll fuck him tonight so I can get the last of what I need to send Lisa all the way crazy.

The pictures Chanel took of us together at the club last night while I was at his table popping bottles was sure to drive her crazy. But I had even more in store for her ass.

I thought about taking a cat nap before getting ready for the day party down at Layla Lounge, but since I was pressed for time, I decided to get in the shower and wash my hair. I needed to change my look tonight. Now that I'd let my hair grow back, I had more options to work with. I was so tired of everyone comparing me to Lauren London, I wore my hair curly more often now. I mean she was cute, fly, and all that, but I liked to have my own identity. She even had my damn dimples, so lately I'd been trying to switch up my look to keep the fellas guessing.

Getting out of the shower, I dried off and put on some of

my smell goods. I then went to my closet to decide what to wear. Since it was hot outside, I decided on my hot pink Betsey Johnson fitted tube dress and my yellow Louboutins. It was eighty degrees outside and I couldn't wait to look like Spring.

"Panties or no panties," I said to myself then looked in the mirror. "Fuck the panties. It's easier access anyway."

Needing to coat my stomach, I thought it would be wise to get something to eat before I left. After walking downstairs and into the kitchen, to my surprise, Marisol and my father were in the foyer about to leave out together.

What the fuck is he doing here? I thought. I hadn't even noticed his car outside.

"You still messing with him, are you serious?" I asked, surprised to see my father and Marisol getting along.

"Didn't we just talk about you being disrespectful," Marisol snapped. "I didn't hear you speak to your father."

"Wassup, Rich. You that nigga, I gotta give it to ya." I laughed before walking past them and into the kitchen. Unfortunately, within seconds they were both on my heels.

"Denie, who do you think you're talkin' to, and where the hell do you think you're goin' dressed like that? This isn't Miami. You need to put some damn clothes on," Rich preached as if I was really gonna listen.

I ignored him as I made a bowl of fruit salad.

"You think you can manipulate every woman in your life. I used to be gullible and hang onto your every word, but I'm on to you now. Marisol, I thought you were stronger than that. How can he kill your husband and then it be all good? Wow." I shook my head back and forth.

Marisol looked like she wanted to jump on me, until Rich held her back.

"Why do you keep throwin' jabs?" Rich questioned. "How long are you gonna make me pay for hurtin' you? I'm sorry. I just want my daughter back."

"Whatever," I replied, trying to stay strong. There was no way I was gonna let that nigga see me cry.

"Let me tell you something little girl. I'm your mother, and this is my house and you will respect me and whatever comes with it. I've done too much to try and make things right. You will do as I say, or you'll see how strong I can be, so try me. For your information, I know everything about your father and Carlos, so no one has to try and hold it over Rich's head anymore."

"Let me guess. It was Jade's fault, or Lisa's fault, hell, maybe Trixie did it. You think you know, huh." I laughed then sashayed myself past them and went back upstairs to my room.

Rich looked so hurt, but his ass deserved it. I was glad when I finally heard the front door close, so I could eat my fruit salad in peace. Moments later, my cell phone rang from an unknown number.

"Hello."

"You have a pre-paid call from a federal prison." The operator went on and on with instructions on what to do and if I wanted to accept or decline the call. I decided to press 0.

"Man, what's up? Why you ain't write me back yet?" Nelson asked.

No bitchassness allowed was my new motto. I definitely wasn't in any mood for his whining.

"Well, hello to you, too, Nelson. How are you doing?" I said in a sarcastic tone.

"I'm sorry baby, I just miss you so much."

I rolled my eyes in my head. "Did you get the money I put on your books?"

"Yes, I did. Thanks baby. Did you get a chance to take my mother that cash last week?"

"Yes, I took your mother $100 for her phone bill and gave her some money to play her numbers."

"I appreciate that. When do you think you gonna make it down here? I ain't seen you in almost two months."

"I don't know."

"Stan's right here, he wanna know if you talked to Chanel. He's been calling her, but she ain't been answering his calls."

"Don't do that. I ain't got shit to do with Chanel and Stan."

"She ain't talked to her," I heard Nelson say to keep the peace.

He knew I didn't play that shit.

As he continued to talk, it was the longest ten minutes of my life. I listened to him complain about how much he needed to see me and how much he loved me and finally the phone went dead. Luckily, he couldn't call back for another thirty minutes. Don't get me wrong, I loved Nelson to death, he was my first true love, but he also left me out here when I needed him most. What made him any different from my father? He'd caught gun and drug charges and left me out here with no one to love. I did my part as much as I could, but a part of me was angry with him and that's something he just didn't understand.

After that draining conversation, I texted Chanel to let her know I was about to leave to pick her up when someone buzzed at the gate. I wasn't expecting company, so I wondered who it could be. I looked on the surveillance camera to see who it was.

Who the fuck is this fine-ass dude in that Bentley, I thought looking at the monitor.

"Yes, how can I help you?"

"Is Marisol home?" he asked.

"No, she isn't. Is there anything I can help you with?"

"Yo' who am I speakin' wit'?"

"I'm gonna buzz you in so you can see for yourself." I flirted.

Before he made it to the door, I fixed my cleavage and hiked up my dress a little. Dude was so fine I could fuck him in a heartbeat. Once I opened the door, his eyes dropped right to my breast.

I smiled. "So, who can I tell Marisol came by."

"My name is Javier," he informed. "Now, you ready to tell me yo' name, Ma?"

"I'm Naomi, her roommate. Are y'all dating or something?"

"No, sweetheart, we like family. We grew up together."

"Oh, how old are you?" I asked. He looked young, but I had to be sure.

"I'm thirty-two, why? You like what you see or somethin'?"

"I might. You from around here?"

"Naw, I'm from up top," he replied.

"I was on my way out to this day party with one of my friends, you tryna hang out? I can show you how we do it in DC."

He shrugged his shoulders. "Why not? I ain't doing shit."

"Okay, you driving though," I mentioned.

"Naw, I might have to dip out early, so I'll just follow you."

"Okay, scared boy."

"Whatever."

He smiled at me, exposing his left dimple. He was fly as hell and iced out, two things that I liked. He might've been like family to Marisol, but he was no family of mine. Those plans I had with Cornell later today might have to wait. Cornell was business, Javier was definitely gonna be pleasure.

Chapter 10

"Damn, girl you look sexy as shit."

"Well, take your clothes off and show me you miss this good pussy."

Makin' my way across the room, all my clothes were off before I even made it to the bed. I stopped in front of her as my throbbin' dick stood at attention.

"Come, let me touch your tonsils," I said.

Gettin' on her knees, she twirled her long tongue around the tip before takin' my entire dick in her mouth...Superhead style. I wondered if she had any reflexes in her mouth, the shit felt so good. The slurpin' sounds and the tight feelin' of her jaws quickly made my eyes roll to the back of my head. She sucked my dick wit' passion, which before long made me wanna cum. As much as I tried to hold back, I couldn't. Seconds later, I bust all in her mouth.

"You like that daddy," she said, finally comin' up for air.

"I love it. Now, come get on top and show me how you missed this dick."

Jumpin' on top, she began to rotate her hips in a slow circular motion before suddenly moving up and down like a professional Polo player. As she picked up the pace, I watched her phat, red ass bounce up against my thighs.

"That's right, make it rain on this dick, cum for me baby."

Suddenly, her pussy began to tighten and her breathin' increased.

"Ahh, Rich I'm about to cum. Ahh I'm cumming," she moaned.

"That's right cum on this dick bitch, cum all on this dick."

Her moans were so seductive there was no way we weren't about to go another round. We ended up fuckin' into the wee hours of the mornin' before finally passin' out.

★★★★★★★★★★★★★★

"Daddy, Daddy! You spent the night," my daughter said early the next morning. She jumped on the bed excited to see me.

"Hey, Juanita, baby. Where's mommy?" I asked after I noticed I was in the bed alone.

"Her downstairs cooking."

"Say 'she's downstairs, not her'. Okay?"

"Okay, Daddy."

"You wanna go to the mall wit' Daddy today? I wanna buy you a few things."

Since I still hadn't used First Lady's credit card, it was time to do some serious splurgin'.

"Yeah! Mommy my daddy is taking me with him to the store!" she yelled when Trixie walked through the door.

"That's great, Nita," Trixie replied then placed a tray over my body.

Obviously still excited, it wasn't long before Juanita ran out the room, leavin' the two of us alone.

"Wow Trixie, breakfast in bed."

She smiled. "Yeah, you put it down last night, so I had to repay you this morning."

"Damn, steak and eggs, my favorite, too."

"Yeah, you see…I remembered."

After I ate breakfast and gettin' myself together, I gave Juanita a bath and got her dressed. By the time I finished, Trixie was back in bed naked and wantin' more. However, no matter how good Trixie was in bed, there was only so much I could take of her in one day. Even though I was back wit' Marisol, there was somethin' about Trixie that I just couldn't get enough of. It was foul to be cheatin' on someone who cared about me once again, but what could I say. I was a typical man…weak when it came to pussy. A simple visit to see my daughter had turned into a full blown sex marathon wit' someone I vowed to never fuck again. It wasn't planned, but as good as that shit was, I wasn't complainin'.

"Trix, I'ma see you later on."

She looked at me sideways. "You could at least give me some since you ain't buying me nothing at the mall."

"It's not about you, it's about my daughter."

"You weren't saying that shit last night while you were clogging my throat," she shot back.

"You right, but I'm sayin' it now. I'm about to bounce."

"Well, I need some money."

Suddenly, our happy rekindled romance had just hit a sour note. "Man, I ain't givin' you shit. I'm takin' Juanita to the mall…nothin' more."

"Well, you ain't taking her anywhere if you don't give me any money."

I couldn't believe she'd gone there. "Bitch, you trippin'. See, this is why I don't like fuckin' you. As soon as you get dick, your ass always start actin' stupid. Here I am tryin' to be a better father and you tryin' to fuck that up."

"You ain't shit, Rich. You're not gonna be sleeping with me and everyone else and not give me any money. I don't know who the hell you think I am, but you know I don't fuck for free. I never have."

"Well Trix, your ass just took one for the team because I'm not givin' you a dime."

Just when she got the balls to talk shit to me the doorbell rang.

"Who is that?"

Instead of answerin' me, she ran downstairs to see who it was, and I was right behind her. I wanted to make sure that it wasn't some nigga. Hell, for all I knew it could've been that young Lil' John lookin' nigga comin' for some get back. When Trixie looked through the small window by the door, then opened it, I couldn't believe who was standin' there.

"What the fuck are you doing here?" Trixie questioned.

"Grandma put me out, so I caught a cab here. Wow, I would think you would be a lot happier to see your first born," her daughter, Toya answered.

"You can't just pop up here when you feel like it," Trixie said.

"Oh, now I see why the long face. You got company."

The attention all of a sudden was directed toward me. I hadn't seen Toya in so long. She had really grown up, big stomach and all.

"Wait a minute, you're pregnant?" Trixie asked wit' a dumbfounded look.

"Naw, I just swallowed a watermelon. See, if you played mommy with both of your daughters, then you would know what was going on in my life," Toya said as she dragged in her bags. "And don't get mad at grandma because I made her swear not to tell you."

Trixie placed her hands on her hips. "So, what makes you think you can just come here, especially now that you're knocked up?"

"Cuz you got the space and you my mother, egg donor, whatever the fuck you want to call yourself these days," Toya responded.

"Hold on, Toya. Now, be a little more respectful to your mother," I interjected. It was like Lisa and Denie all over again and I just couldn't take it any longer.

"You need to mind your business," Toya snapped.

I wanted to slap the shit out of her smart-ass mouth. "Look, I know it's been a while since you've seen me. We've never even sat down and had a real conversation, but I damn sure don't remember you being so disrespectful."

"Rich, right?" Toya asked like she couldn't remember. When I shook my head, she continued. "Normally, I would have a comeback, but I actually wanna shake your hand. I hear you're the one who killed that bastard Mike."

"Toya, don't start," Trixie interrupted.

"No, I don't know if Rich really knows the real Trixter," Toya fired back.

Trixie tried talkin' over Toya like she was tryin' to hide somethin'. I silenced them both because I wanted to hear what Toya had to say.

"Hold up…first of all Miss Lady, I ain't kill nobody. Secondly, what's your beef wit' your mother?" I was curious as hell.

"She put me out after she came home from work one night and caught Mike on top of me. That's my beef. No matter how much I tried to tell her he was abusing me, she never listened. When he got me pregnant, she was done. After she took me to get an abortion, she dropped me off at my grandmother's house and never turned back."

At that moment it looked like Toya wanted to cry.

"So, after having one abortion, you went and got pregnant again? That was smart," Trixie commented.

Toya shook her head. "I sure did. At least my baby is gonna love me!"

"Damn, how long are you gonna throw that shit in my face, Toya? I'm sorry that I put you out all because of Mike. I'm sorry I didn't believe you," Trixie said as tears began to race down her face.

I'm sure it felt like she was bein' attacked by all of the

skeletons in her closet.

"No matter how many times you say that you're sorry, it doesn't change how I feel. It doesn't erase my scars."

All of a sudden this hard-ass mutant turned into a soft little girl who obviously needed a hug.

One thing I knew was I didn't sign up for this shit. I was officially ready to go. If I wanted to deal wit' a hard headed teenager, I would've been tryin' to reconcile wit' Denie.

"Well, I guess y'all have some catchin' up to do, so I'ma go ahead and roll out."

After listenin' to them go back and forth a few more rounds, Juanita and I finally left and headed out to Tyson's Corner Mall.

Juanita was the spittin' image of both me and Denie. She was such a cute little girl and her curly hair that Trixie let run wild wit' a headband always got me attention wit' the ladies. As soon as we got in the car, the flood of questions started. She was very talkative, and asked damn near every question her little brain could think of until we arrived at the mall thirty minutes later.

We started out at Nordstrom in Tyson's 1. After buyin' her a cute pair of studded flip flops and a shirt, we made our way to the men's department so I could get me a new pair of Gucci loafers. I was so glad that First Lady still hadn't cancelled the cards. It would've been embarrassing to get denied. Once Juanita got her a Ladybug Pillow Pet from a kiosk in the middle of the mall, we stopped at a few more places, before I decided to go to the Apple store to check out the latest gadgets. Both me and my baby girl fell absolutely in love with the new Ipad, so since this shoppin' spree wasn't on my dime, I bought two of them muthafuckas along with two cases and a car charger.

Fuck you, First Lady, I thought. *Consider this shit rent money to stay up in my crib.*

When it was time to eat, we headed across the street to Tyson's 2, to get her a real meal. Even though Juanita had been begging for chicken nuggets since we first arrived, I wanted her to have some real food. We ended up goin' to one of my favorite restaurants called Wildfire. Of course we couldn't be in Tyson's 2 without hittin' the Juicy store. I ended up gettin' her a cute little bathin' suit, along with a t-shirt that ironically read, *I Heart Dad* and a charm bracelet. Once we got upstairs to the restaurant, it was a long wait, so I slipped the waitress a twenty dollar bill to seat us right away. In this case I couldn't use the credit card. Back in the day it would've been a hundred, but these days the twenty would have to do.

Lunch was cool wit' my baby girl and I actually enjoyed being wit' her. As we were leavin' the restaurant all the waitresses had fallen in love wit' Juanita. That girl was a chick magnet, so I could definitely get used to hangin' out wit' her. Gatherin' her bag, I grabbed Juanita's hand and started out into the mall. As we walked, a familiar laugh immediately caught my attention. I got the shock of my life when I suddenly turned around.

"What the fuck are you doin' wit' my daughter?" I yelled.

"Rich, mind your business, I'm good," Denie fired back.

I could tell she was embarrassed, but there was no way I was cool wit' her bein' wit' that nigga, Javier.

"So, Rich is yo' pops?" Javier shot Denie a shockin' look.

Denie frowned. "Hell no, I told you my father died."

"Denie, what the fuck are you talkin' about? Yeah, that's my daughter, nigga. Don't you think she's a little too young to be fuckin' wit' you?" I questioned.

"I didn't say anything about you fuckin' wit' my sister, so don't worry about what the fuck me and Naomi got goin' on," Javier added.

"Naomi? Her name is Denie. So, what y'all a damn couple...y'all fuckin?" I hated talkin' that way in front of Juanita again, but in this case, it was necessary. "Nigga, if you lay hands on my daughter I'll kill you!"

Javier bit his bottom lip. "Yo', don't be sendin' me no

damn threats. It looks like yo' daughter wants to be touched, and I believe I'm the dude to scratch that itch."

"He's just jealous. He wish his pockets were on swole like yours, boo," Denie instigated.

She knew how to push my buttons. The mention of my financial situation sent me over the edge every time. As Denie switched her Gucci, Louis Vuitton and Saks bags into her other hand, I got even more irritated.

"Don't worry about my bread little girl. If you keep bein' disrespectful, I'm gonna embarrass your ass in front of your so-called man," I warned.

"Put yo' hands on her and see what happens," Javier threatened.

Wit' my gun in the car, it was a good reason why I didn't have it on me because both of my daughters would'a witnessed me commit murder.

"Da-d-deeey!"

I had to get my temper under control when Juanita started to cry.

"Go ahead and save your new little girl because I'm good. I'm grown and not a concern of yours anymore. Come on Javier, fuck him, he ain't worth you going to jail," Denie said.

As they walked away, I noticed we'd started to gain attention causin' me to deal wit' the situation later. Everything happened for a reason, because God knows if I didn't have Juanita wit' me, Denie would've had the taste slapped out of her mouth and Javier would be joinin' his fuckin' sister.

Beyond pissed, I was in no mood for kids, so when I got in the car I called Trixie to let her know I had to drop Juanita off at her hair salon. She knew by my tone not to give me a hard time. The next phone call I made was to Marisol. The reason Denie went to go live wit' her in the first place was to get herself together. She was supposed to be guidin' her in the right direction. I wanted to know ASAP how the fuck she'd let this happen. I called Marisol's phone three times, but her voicemail kept pickin' up. After the fourth time, she finally answered.

"Rich, what's up. I'm handling business," she said irritated.

"Fuck your business! You were supposed to do a better job raisin' my daughter than I could, and now she's out fuckin' Javier for clothes!"

"What the hell are you talking about?"

"I'm out Tyson's wit' Juanita and I bumped into Denie and Javier."

"You've got to be kidding me. How the hell do they know each other?"

"You tell me, them your peoples."

"Hold on, I'm about to call Denie right now on the three way."

She called Denie's phone, but there was no answer.

"Hold on, I'll call Javier, but don't say anything," Marisol said, clickin' over.

Javier answered on the first ring.

"Oh, so now I hear from you. It's mighty funny I've been callin' you ever since that night we met up and you been duckin' my calls. What let me guess…yo' boy Rich called to tell you he seen me wit' your roommate?"

"That's not my roommate asshole, that's my daughter. How the fuck did you meet her?"

"I came past yo' house and Naomi told me she was your roommate."

"Her fucking name is Denie. Are you fucking my daughter?" Marisol questioned.

"Man, I ain't about to be interrogated when you can't even stand up for yo' so called friend. Did you find out if yo' dude Rich knows what happened to my sister?"

"Jade don't have shit to do with what we're talking about right now," Marisol shot back.

"Well, I'ma continue seein' Denie, Naomi, whoever, so don't call me wit' that nonsense. Oh, and tell yo' boy Rich, she got some good ass pussy." Javier cracked up laughing.

"Nigga, when I catch you, you're dead!" I yelled, hopin'

he heard me before hangin' up.

My temper was at a point where it couldn't be controlled. Now that Javier knew Denie was my daughter, I feared for her life.

If he suspects that I killed his sister, there's no tellin' what his plans for Denie will be.

Chapter 11

Lisa

God must've heard my prayers. After all this time, Cornell was finally coming to visit me, which I couldn't have been more excited about. Not only did I miss him dearly, I also wanted him to give me another chance. He was all that I had left in this world, and I definitely needed him to know that. Maybe if he saw me trying to get help in this place he would see the person that he once fell for.

Making my way over to my mirror, I looked at myself and frowned. There was no way he was going to see me like this. I had to make a way to get myself in order before he got there and I knew just the person to call to get me all glam and fabulous. Grabbing my cell phone from my top drawer, I decided to give Jermaine a call.

"Chello sista!" he greeted.

"Hey Jermaine, how did you know it was me?"

"Your number came up silly. Girl, you ain't been here in a month of Sundays. What's going on with? What's going on with your hair?"

"I've been through some things. I was admitted in a hospital. It's a long story that I don't feel like getting into right now, but I need you, like in the next twenty minutes."

"Are you serious? I'm twirling right now. I had me a good night at Tradewinds and then came home with the trade. He's fine as wine and I'm not trying to leave him. You lucky I answered my phone for you this early on a Sunday."

"Jermaine, please do me this favor. My hair hasn't been done in months and Cornell is on his way up here. There's no way he can see me like this."

"But girl, I'm all the way out Gaithersburg."

After a little more begging and pleading, I finally convinced Jermaine to peel away from his date and come to my rescue. He took over an hour to get to me and I was stressed out the entire time thinking Cornell was gonna get to the hospital first. Jermaine walked in my room colorful as ever. He looked so cute with his red and white Gucci outfit. Of course he couldn't walk in the building without his matching Gucci sunglasses.

He studied me and the room a few seconds before giving me a huge hug.

"Okay, Boo-Boo, what's really going on? This is a crazy house. How in the world did you end up in here?"

"Like I said, it's a long story and I really don't wanna talk about it."

"Well, I know you ain't letting that fine- ass ball player come to see you up in here are you?"

"Jermaine, how am I gonna be able to see him if he doesn't come up here?" I asked.

"I guess you right." Jermaine played with my hair that had grown almost to my shoulder. "Oh my goodness. Look at this head of yours. When's the last time you washed it? Before I could reply, he was already on another question. "Girl, why didn't you tell me Denie wasn't really your daughter? Denie's been coming to get her hair done over the past two months and always be running her mouth like crazy. She's going around telling all your business."

"Jermaine, I hate to be rude, but I really don't feel like hearing what that bitch Denie or anybody else has to say about me. I'm already under enough stress."

"Chile, I understand." He walked over and grabbed his bag, then pulled out some Influance shampoo, conditioner, his flat iron and other hair necessities. "Girl, it's like Fort Knox up in here. They weren't even trying to let me bring this stuff. Luckily, they didn't see the shears or my razor that I hid," he advised.

After giving me a hard time about taking better care of my hair and filling me in on the shop drama, Jermaine definitely came to the rescue and had me looking like a million bucks forty-five minutes later. He'd cut my hair into a really cute choppy bob. I loved it and I was sure that Cornell would, too.

"Thank you so much Jermaine. You know I'm good for the payment as soon as I get out of here."

"Yeah, don't be trying to skip town when you get out," he joked.

After Jermaine left to go back home and finish entertaining his company, I was already starting to feel better about myself. As I looked in the mirror, my self esteem instantly lifted. There she was, the old Lisa. Even though I'd lost a lot of weight, I felt better about how I looked. I wanted Cornell to remember me the way I was before he caught me pumping poison into my body. Cornell was what I needed to get better. Maybe he could even help me get out of this place.

As I envisioned happy thoughts of me and Cornell, I suddenly drifted off to sleep. Nurse Betty woke me up to have some lab work done about twenty minutes later, and as my luck would have it, Cornell knocked on the door while I was having my blood drawn. I was pissed that he had to see that. Since I wanted him to have a vision of me being healthy, I was disappointed.

"Hey, Lisa," Cornell said, peeking in the doorway to see if it was okay to come in.

I was so happy to see him. "Hey, Cornell. You can come on in, she's just about done," I said giving Nurse Betty the 'hurry the fuck up' look.

Cornell looked better than ever. He'd let his beard grow, which made him look quite handsome. He also looked damn good in a white Burberry polo-style shirt, distressed jeans and Louis Vuitton patent leather tennis shoes. He had a fresh scent that made me want to pull the needle out my arm and grab him.

When Nurse Betty was finally done, she quickly left the room and closed the door behind her. Almost immediately, I got up off the bed and gave him a hug. His embrace was something well overdue and strongly needed. Before we unlocked, I gazed into his eyes and tried to give him a kiss, but he backed away. It was an awkward silence for a few moments until he finally spoke.

"So, how you feelin'?" he finally asked.

"I feel really good," I lied with a smile.

"Well, you look good?"

"Thanks babe. So, I see you've been playing well. I've been watching your games. I'm so excited that you all won the other night. It's actually surprising. The Celtics are a good team."

"Thanks. I've actually been talkin' to a couple of other teams and might be movin' when the season is over. It's really not workin' for me here."

"What do you mean it's not working?" I questioned. In my mind I was asking, *what about us?*

"I'm not really feelin' my coach and let's face it. That shit was pure luck that we won that game. Everybody knows we're not gonna advance any further. I'm tryin' to get a ring, and I can't get that here."

I wanted to say, 'nice confidence in your team', but he was probably right.

"Stay here. I can give you a ring," I said jokingly, but he knew I was serious. I guess that's why he didn't find it funny.

He avoided the question. "So Lisa, how have you been holdin' up now that Juan's gone?"

I'm sure that was his way of addressing the elephant in

the room. He really wanted to ask me, why I was in a mental institution.

"Cornell, if you really want to know why I'm in here just ask."

"Okay, why are you in here? First you snortin' coke, now this? Man, I just don't get it. When we met you seemed so strong."

I sat back on the bed. "Cornell, don't judge me. You have no idea what I've been through in my life."

"I'm not judgin' you. I'm just bein' real with you. All I ask is that you do the same."

"Cornell, after we broke up and Juan died I had a mental break down. I'd experienced so much with Rich that I was on my last straw. I'm in a better place now though."

"Well, let me just get to the point and cut through the chase. The reason why I came is because I wanted to let you know that I've moved on with my life and you can't keep callin' me like you have. Reachin' out to any and everyone to try and get my attention is causin' issues for me."

"What do you mean? Don't try and make me out to be some type of stalker or something!"

"Come on Lisa. I ain't never in my life had a woman call up to the Wizard's head office requestin' to talk to me. Not even a fan. I don't need the organization in my business gettin' caught up in your drama."

"My drama? Are you kidding me?"

"Let me finish Lisa…"

"No, I'm not gonna allow you to paint me as this obsessive…"

"Well, what do you call it? Man, the media is havin' a field day with me dealin' with you. Because of you and your husband's drama, I've lost business deals. It's not worth it to me. What we had I enjoyed, but all this has to stop."

My heart was full of pain. Me getting dolled up and trying to look the part didn't matter to him. He obviously had his mind made up, but I wasn't gonna let him dismiss me that easily. I loved him. My mother and Rich didn't give a fuck about me anymore, so there was no way I was gonna allow all of the good times we shared just go up in smoke.

"Cornell, I love you, and I'm not trying to destroy your life. I just need a friend. I need you, Cornell. You're all I have left."

"Come on Lisa, don't put that all on me. You have family. If I'm all you have, then I don't know what else to tell you."

"How am I supposed to take that? Remember when I didn't want to give us a chance and kept pushing you away. Now, do you see why? I love hard and I've lost everyone that I care about. Both of my children died in one year."

"And I'm sorry about that, but do you know how much my life has been turned upside down with headlines like…NBA Star Involved with Drug Lord's Wife and Cornell Willis Drives his Jump-Off to the Crazy House."

"That's enough!" I screamed.

"Don't you think I took a risk comin' to see you today? But out of respect for Juan, I thought it was best that I came to have this conversation face to face."

"Don't you dare speak my son's name! I looked for you at the funeral, you weren't even there! And you called yourself a fucking friend!"

No longer able to hold back my pain, my eyes suddenly started to fill up with the tears. Just when I thought things couldn't get any worse, the devil herself walked in.

"Hi Lisa, am I interrupting something?"

My face immediately turned cold. "As a matter of fact you are Marisol."

What the hell was she doing here? I hated her even more now for what she'd done. Making me look like a fool all these years by raising her disrespectful-ass daughter while she played Auntie Marisol the entire time was fucked up. I could never let her back in my life again. That bitch was the last person I wanted to see me in a mental hospital, but I promised myself that before it was all over, I was going to show that bitch crazy.

"Lisa, are you gonna introduce me to your friend?" As Marisol smiled with her straight teeth that shit made me want to knock all them motherfuckers right out of her mouth.

Who the hell got all dolled up to come and visit somebody at a hospital? She had on a pair of black leggings with a cropped studded shirt that stopped just above her hips. I'm sure she'd worn the Nikki Minaj inspired outfit just to expose her ass. The six-inch spiked Christian Louboutin heels were a dead giveaway that she needed some attention or she was on her way to the club. With her hair really wild and curly, she had a nerve to have on the same oversized diamond hoop earrings that Carlos and Rich bought both of us while we were on vacation in St. Thomas.

"I guess you didn't go to church today, dressed like a hooker," I stated with a devious smirk.

"Wow, Lisa. Let's play nice." She reached over to shake Cornell's hand. "Hi, I'm Marisol, and you are?"

"I'm Cornell," he said, admiring Marisol's physique.

"Oh, so you're 'The Cornell Willis?' I didn't know you and Lisa were still dating."

"Umm, well we're not, I just came to visit," Cornell informed.

"Mind your business, whore. What the hell are you doing here anyway?" I snapped.

"Well, I've been trying to call you, but you haven't been accepting my calls. I was gonna ask if you didn't mind getting me tickets for the next playoff game, but I guess since Cornell is here I can ask him myself."

I quickly shook my head. "Oh, hell no, bitch you're delusional if you think Cornell is gonna give you anything."

"Well, what's your name again…Marisol?" Cornell asked. He ignored the face that I didn't approve.

"Yes," Marisol answered.

"Put my number in your phone and I'll make sure I get my assistant to get you a couple of tickets."

"Are you serious? Thank you so much. Lisa, I wish you

could go. Do you think you can get a pass to come out on Wednesday?" Marisol taunted. She quickly grabbed her phone and typed in Cornell's number.

"Bitch, I can't believe you're gonna..." I tried to say.

"Look, I ain't tryin' to be caught up in any drama, so I'ma bounce. I'll be in touch for the tickets Marisol, and Lisa take care of yourself," Cornell said, then turned around.

I held out my hand. "But wait Cornell. We still need to talk. I'm not done."

"Well, I am," he continued.

Just as Cornell left the room, he took my heart with him. I wanted to kill Marisol with my bare hands for ruining my last chance to fight for the man I loved. The bitch even had a nerve to grin as she watched the door slam. When she directed her attention back to me, for some reason I knew by her body language what she was here for.

Chapter 12

Marisol

"Let's just cut to the chase, Lisa. Were you fucking my husband?"

"Oh, like you were fucking mine." She stared at me for a few seconds before continuing. "How dare you question me after you had me raise your pain in the ass, deranged daughter?"

"Well, I had to do what I had to do. Besides, what you fail to realize is that everybody knows you never gave a fuck about Denie, so stop saying you raised her. All you cared about was your precious Juan."

"So, how's it going with Denie now anyway?" Lisa laughed as if she was trying to hit me with a cheap shot.

"It's actually going really good. Denie will be enrolling in school at F.I.T. for the fall semester. She won't be fucked up like you. Look at how your thirsty-ass fucked up your son's life. No matter how much we tried to tell you not to let that boy get involved in the streets when Rich got locked up, you still had to get all that material shit just to keep up with the Joneses."

"Fuck you bitch! Don't even speak my son's name out of

your mouth!" Lisa shouted.

Knowing I'd hit a nerve, I went in for the kill. I wanted to push every button I could to get the truth about Carlos out of her. She was so weak, I knew exactly what to do to get the information I needed.

"So, how does it feel now since you don't have anyone, and I have everything you want? I have my kids, your ex-husband whenever I need some dick, and money."

It looked like she wanted to cry. "I'll be alright."

"Yeah, looks like your life is going swell. I mean, think about it…I just gave your little NBA baller my number. He thinks I want tickets, but I'll have that little boy eating out the palm of my hands in a week."

"You're so fucking desperate."

"Never desperate sweetheart," I replied. "Now, you still failed to answer my question. Were you fucking my husband?" I made sure to get a little closer so she knew I was serious.

"You damn right, I was fucking the shit out of him. Actually, he spent his last day on Earth with yours truly. When you needed your husband while your daughter's hair was falling out, he was fucking me."

She definitely caught me off guard with the comment about Mia. The old Lisa would've never said such an evil thing about my daughter. As I looked around the room I laid my eyes on a corny-ass snow globe sitting on Lisa's table that someone must've bought her during the holidays. I envisioned it in my hand and then smacking it across Lisa's head. That bitch had to go and if it wasn't for the nurses knowing I was in her room right now she would be dead. I had to work out a plan to make that happen, but couldn't be sloppy Even though her words stung, I had to play it cool in order to get the information I needed about my husband, at least as cool as I could be.

"So, fucking you got my husband killed, huh?"

"Here you are responsible for my son's death, and now you are trying to put Carlos' blood on my hands."

"You just said he spent his last day with you, you dumb

bitch. So if you were the last person he fucked that means you were the last person he saw. Now, I'm gonna ask you again, did you have anything to do with my husband's death."

"I'm the wrong one to be interrogating," Lisa responded.

"That ain't what Rich said. He actually told me you killed *my* husband. So please do me a favor and be a woman and let that shit come out your mouth so I can put you six feet deep.

Lisa laughed. "And you just called me a dumb bitch. The fact that you believe Rich makes you look stupid as shit."

When I tried to approach her, Lisa started going off. "Stay the fuck away from me!"

When Lisa opened her mouth and spit a huge wad of salvia in my face, my mind went to another place. The first thing I did was give her two quick Floyd Mayweather style jabs across her face. Of course I knew she would grab for my hair. The entire time she held onto my locks, I used her face as a punching bag by landing several uppercuts. Lisa couldn't get out of the headlock I had her in at first until she bit my arm, causing me to lose my grip. She even got in a couple of scratches, but that shit was minor compared to the last punch I gave her across the nose. Even though blood was everywhere, I still wasn't done with her ass. Pulling Lisa off the bed, I took that bitch and mopped her ass all over that room until several security guards and nurses burst inside.

"She attacked me. Oh my God she's crazy!" I faked, as they pulled us a part.

"She's lying, she's lying, I'm not crazy!" Lisa responded as the nurses held her down and began sedating her. She yelled all different kind of obscenities before falling into a comatose state a few minutes later.

"I apologize for this. We thought that Ms. Sanchez was fit to have visitors unsupervised. She appeared to be doing better. She's you're cousin correct?" one of the nurses inquired.

"Yes. I can't believe the state that Lisa's in. I didn't know it was this bad," I said, grabbing my purse from the floor. "You all are just as crazy as she is if you let her ass out of here!"

"Don't worry, incidents like this, go into her file," the nurse advised.

"Good."

My shirt was torn, but that was the least of my worries. Figuring out how I was gonna take Lisa out while she was in the hospital was all I could think about as I got on the elevator to leave. Security even walked me out as if I really needed them. I guess they really thought I was scared, but they had no idea what I was capable of. Lisa was gonna pay before it was all over with.

Making my way to the car, I couldn't help but think how after all that just went down, I still couldn't get Lisa to admit to Carlos' death. But there was no doubt in my mind that she'd actually pulled the trigger. Rich's story was way too detailed for him to be lying. All that bitch ever did was deny everything and point the finger at someone else. Even though I wanted to hear her say that shit to finally give me some type of closure, it still didn't matter. It's not like that visit had spared her life. She was gonna die regardless. As I drove away from the hospital and made my way home, I couldn't help but wonder why Denie was convinced that Rich was involved though. I wasn't sure if she was on get back or what. That situation was something I needed to get down to the bottom of, and hopefully if Denie could be found she would calmy sit down with me and set the record straight.

Denie had been missing in action for a couple of days since I found out she'd been seeing Javier. Since he thought it was cool to continue to mess around with her knowing she was my daughter, I definitely had a bone to pick with his ass. All I could hope was that he wasn't on some type of get back shit because of his sister. If that was the case, he could expect an all out war. He wasn't gonna fuck with my family and get away with it

As I drove down Martin Luther King Avenue, I made a couple of calls to my partners in New York to see if they'd seen Javier. Surprisingly, no one had seen him in almost a week, which immediately had me concerned. It made me wonder if he'd taken my daughter somewhere without her consent.

Mentally I was drained and needed a moment of relaxation. I didn't know who to trust anymore and didn't want to fall vulnerable to Rich. I needed to stay strong. Once I pulled up to the house Maria frantically ran out to greet me and started rambling to me in Spanish.

"What's wrong Maria?" I asked in a concerned tone.

"Ayuda! Ayuda! No Respira!"

"Speak English Maria. I can't understand!"

"Mia, she's not breathing!"

It felt like my heart instantly stopped. "What? Call 911!"

****

I paced in the emergency room at Children's Hospital for what seemed like hours with no answers about my daughter's progress. All I knew so far was that Mia had gone into cardiac arrest, which had me on pins and needles. Trying not to think negatively, I constantly told myself that my daughter was a survivor so there was no reason to be alarmed. Not to mention, she'd been in remission one time, so whatever this setback was wouldn't keep her down for long. Trying to remain calm, I prayed my daughter would pull through as she always did.

With several scratches all over my face and neck, I'm sure the nurses and doctors wondered what type of hell I'd been through. I just hoped they didn't think it had anything to do with Mia. With Maria at the house with Carmen and Rich on his way, I was all alone to deal with the unknown.

Reaching in my purse, I pulled out my cell phone and tried to reach Denie again. I'd been trying to call to let her know what was going on, but she still didn't answer. As I left a message, Rich rushed in with great concern.

"I was on my way out Baltimore, but I tried to get here as soon as I could. Any word yet?" he asked.

I shook my head. "No, not yet."

He clutched my chin then moved my face back and forth. "What the hell happened to you?"

"Your ex wife, but don't worry she looks worse."

Just as I was ready to go into detail, Mia's doctor finally came out. I was so glad he happened to be on call at the hospital. He'd been dealing with Mia's Leukemia right along with me since day one.

"Hello Mrs. Sanchez," he greeted then turned to Rich. "Hello sir. I'm Dr. Friedman, Mia's physician."

"Dr. Friedman, please tell me you have good news," I said.

"Well, we had some complications."

My eyes became larger. "What kind of complications?"

Dr. Friedman paused for a moment. "There's no easy way to say this, Mrs. Sanchez, but I'm afraid we lost Mia. Even though we were able to resuscitate her, we weren't able to control the infection in her blood. I looked at the lab work before coming out here. Unfortunately, when you were here the last time, I suspected that Mia's Leukemia had returned, and it's true. I'm so sorry we tried…"

My body went completely numb for about thirty seconds and I could no longer hear anything the doctor said. After he told me my baby was dead, I could only see his mouth moving, but nothing was coming out. Moments later, I broke down.

"No. Please, no. Not my baby. Not my daughter!"

"Oh my God," Rich whispered as he held me.

Dr. Friedman rubbed my shoulder as well. "Again, Mrs. Sanchez, I'm so sorry. I know this has been a fight for you and your family. If you wanna see her to say your final goodbyes, I'll make that happen as quickly as possible."

"Dr. Friedman, this isn't funny. I don't believe you. What do you mean say my final goodbyes? She can't be gone. How did this happen? It's your fault. You gave her antibiotics. You told me that if it was an infection that it would go away. You told me she was getting better this winter. How could this happen?" I cried.

"Apparently the infection was so aggressive that it didn't respond well to the medication," Dr. Friedman spoke. "Her poor little body just couldn't fight anymore."

Suddenly, I lunged at Dr. Friedman. I was pissed that he'd gotten my hopes up and had me believing that my daughter was gonna survive. Despite me knowing that the cancer had possibly come back, he never told me that this would be the outcome. Smacking him in the face, I wanted him to feel the same pain that I felt as Rich pulled me away.

"Dr. Friedman, she's hurt. Please forgive her," Rich apologized.

"I should've done more. I should've done more," I wailed.

"Don't blame yourself, Mrs. Sanchez, or anyone else. We did all we could," Dr. Friedman replied.

There was no way I could control my emotions as I fell to the floor and sobbed uncontrollably. I then began beating the cold tile until my hands were tomato red.

"Ohhhh noooo. Why, God, why? I prayed to you and trusted you. You took my baby and my husband away from me. Why are you doing this to me?" I sobbed.

Chapter 13

Message 1-

"Denie I know you've disappeared before in the past, but this time shit seems different. No matter what we've gone through, I just want you to know that I love you and I'm worried about you. Damn, would you just answer the phone! We just need to know that you're breathin' and that nigga Javier didn't do shit to you to get back at me. Call me man!" Rich yelled.

Message 2-

"Denie it's Marisol again. I haven't heard from you in over a month, so I desperately need to know that you're okay. I'm worried sick about you and I can't function without knowing you're alright. This shit with Javier is a non-motherfucking factor at this point because there are much bigger issues to deal with. I've been trying to avoid telling you this over the voicemail, but Mia is gone. She's gone Denie, so we need you back home. It's been too long. I'm losing my mind thinking about you. By you not being at your sister's funeral really has me really nervous. Please call me back. We love you.

It was the twentieth message I'd gotten from Marisol, but this was the first time she seemed so hysterical. I'd never seen that side of her before. As far as Rich calling me to death, I really didn't give a fuck. He could kiss my ass and wait on that return call until he was old and gray. No matter how bad I wanted to let Marisol know I was okay, I had to stick to my guns. I'm sure she was upset that I hadn't gone to Mia's funeral, but Marisol needed to realize that I was going to mourn for my little sister in my own way. If I hadn't bothered to come back home for the funeral what made her think that calling me would work either? I loved Mia, and even felt bad that the disease had finally taken her life, but going home meant being interrogated about Javier, and I didn't feel like dealing with that shit. Call me selfish, but it is what it is. Javier made me happy and that's all that mattered to me right now. I finally had someone in my life that made me feel loved. It wasn't just about Javier wining and dining me every night, but he was attentive to my needs and made me feel like I mattered.

It seemed as if the past month had gone by so fast. After coming to New York so he could handle some business, we were supposed to go back to D.C. the following day. But with Javier so busy, we had yet to make it back. To be quite honest, I didn't want to leave anyway, so it wasn't a big issue for me. I looked at it as fate anyway, especially since I'd gotten accepted to The Fashion Institute. Now, I could really be closer to my new man.

Initially, once I found out Javier was Jade's brother it was all about me rebelling against Rich. I knew it would burn my father up that I was with someone he forbid me to see, but once I got to know Javier over these past four weeks, I couldn't help but fall for him. When I used to watch those dating reality shows, I laughed at all the dumb chicks falling in love so easily, so quick. It seemed impossible for them to date a guy for only a day or two and fall head over heels. However, being with Javier made me eat my own words. Not only was he fine, but his sex was off the chain. A bit freakier than I was used to, but still good.

I didn't know how to take it at first, but now I could appreciate his good love making. Javier licked every inch of my body and sucked all the juices from my pussy which wasn't a problem, but it was just how he did it that made my eyebrows rise sometimes. It seemed as if he was down for whatever. What really threw me for a loop was the fact that he had a piercing inserted in his dick that was supposed to stimulate the clitoris during sex. The shit was actually painful and whenever I told him, he always brushed me off. His motto was 'pain is pleasure' which was something I had to get used to if I wanted to be with him. Javier was different from anyone I'd ever slept with, but there was a mystery about him that I enjoyed. He kept my mind off the problems in my life and he made me feel wanted. We'd been together every day since we met and I wasn't about to leave now.

"You still catching Z's, babe," I said, trying to wake Javier up.

He'd been in such a deep, comatose sleep all morning.

I'm ready for our workout, I thought rubbing his arms. Even though it was going on twelve o'clock, I was still geared up for our normal morning sex session.

Opening his eyes, Javier tried to smile, but immediately started coughing uncontrollably. He'd been suffering from a nagging dry cough for days now, and even though I kept telling his ass to go see a doctor, he kept beating me down saying that it was just his allergies.

"You ready for your Zyrtec, boo?"

Like I told him, there was nothing that medicine could do that I couldn't to make him feel better. Javier just laughed at me when I said that, but I meant it. No other girl could come close to the way I fucked him.

"You ain't ready for me?" Javier replied with a half smile. He still looked tired as hell.

"Whatever, it looks like you're still out of it. Rest up, because you're gonna need it."

"Why don't you make me something to eat? I should be

ready after I get some food in my system."

"No problem. Anything to make you feel better. Are you eating in here?"

He nodded his head. "Yeah."

I felt his forehead. "Now, I know you're sick because we never eat in the bedroom, Mr. Clean."

His smile made me melt. All he had to do was let that left dimple peek out at me, and then it was all over. Trying to handle my womanly duties, I slid out of bed, then made my way downstairs to the kitchen to start preparing his lunch. Since Javier was a little under the weather, I decided to open a can of chicken noodle soup, and make a grilled cheese sandwich. Hell, I'd grown up with Lisa cooking for me, and Maria doing everything at Marisol's house, so I didn't know how to make but so much.

Pouring the Progresso soup inside a pot, I turned the stove on then stirred it a bit before suddenly looking around Javier's modern style home. With an all white Italian leather sofa, snow white carpet, expensive paintings and custom window treatments, it wasn't the average bachelor pad. After being with Nelson and a few other dudes with money, I knew what most niggas houses were supposed to look like, but Javier's spot was out of the norm. There were no dirty socks laying around, no water spots on the bathroom mirror and definitely no dishes in the sink. Everything was spotless. When I first walked into the exposed brick loft, I instantly thought his son's mother had helped with the décor because the place definitely had a woman's touch. However, anytime I would ask about her or his son, Javier would become extremely touchy. Both had passed away in a car accident a few years ago, so I decided to leave that subject alone.

After preparing the sandwich, then placing the food in two of Javier's fancy china sets, I made my way back upstairs to serve him in bed. Surprisingly, he was sitting up.

"Come over here and sit on daddy's lap," he flirted, then pulled back the white down comforter to expose his extra large penis.

"Damn, I haven't been gone that long. You're feeling better rather quickly."

Not needing a response, I sat the dishes down before taking off my fuchsia corset and thong set he'd bought me. I knew it was a matter of time before he couldn't resist me in it. My breasts were purchased by Nelson last year and my ass had always been nice and plump, so the reason for his manhood being at attention was understood. Before I made me way over to sit on my man's lap, I decided to put on some Trey Songz to set the mood.

"You missed your, baby?" I asked, climbing on top of him.

"Stop talking and let me get inside of my pussy."

Deep down inside I knew it was wrong for me to have sex with him without a condom, but ever since Rich saw us together at the mall, Javier wanted to prove to me that we wouldn't allow anyone to come between what we had. Not to mention, he wanted to feel all of me. Shit, I wanted to feel all of him, too. It was a decision I had yet to regret.

As I started to ride him, it took me a minute to work is big tool inside of my nest. He wasn't the type that you could just get on and start working. I had to move the tip of his dick around the perimeter of my vagina for few seconds then ease him inside of me, before finally being able to perform.

I rotated my hips in a circular motion. "Who's dick is this?"

"Yours, Ma," Javier replied.

His dick kept jerking as if he was trying to hold back from busting a nut as soon as I picked up the pace. I wasn't ready for our lovemaking to end, so I immediately got up and placed my ass in the air so he could hit it from the back. I knew that when I was on top he couldn't handle it, but that was my favorite position.

Moments later, Javier positioned himself behind me, grabbed my ass with both hands, then dived into my wet pussy. As he pounded me from behind, he always seemed to tap the spots that made me whimper and moan.

"Ahh, Javier. Work this pussy," I purred like a kitten.

I then pulled on my nipples as my firm breasts bounced from side to side. I knew Javier freaky-ass loved it when I pleased myself. As I began tightening my walls, trying to get him to the ultimate climax, Javier pulled out and waited a minute before he tried to enter my ass.

"Uh-uh. No, I don't like that."

"Yo' come on Denie, you suppose to my girl, man. You fuckin' up the mood." Javier layed back on the bed like he had an attitude.

"Just because I don't want you to fuck me in my ass, I'm messing up the mood?" When I got the silent treatment, I started to massage his dick. "Well, let me make it up to you then."

Within seconds, I'd placed his ten –inch dick inside my mouth, then started to move my head up and down at a steady pace. That seemed to calm him down for the moment, but he still appeared to be really upset.

"You like it baby?" I questioned between slurps.

As I worked hard to try and make him feel good, he seemed the least bit interested. Javier ignored me with his eyes closed as my mouth became tired. He was right…the mood had been ruined, but he was going to have to be mad because I was sticking to my guns.

"I guess you don't like it since you're ignoring me."

At that moment, I stopped, laid back, and pulled the covers over my head. There was complete silence for a good fifteen minutes until Javier finally decided to speak up.

"Denie, even though we made a promise not to discuss Rich or Marisol, there's somethin' that's holdin' me back from givin' you my all and I don't wanna do that because I love you."

I quickly turned over. "I don't want you to hold back with me either, especially if it's because of him. I hate that man. Why are you allowing him to come between what we're trying to build?"

"It's just a lot on my mind, Denie. My sister was all I had

left, and I believe Rich killed her. I feel so lost sometimes, I just need answers. "

When Javier started to get emotional, it made me feel sorry for him. I was weak for a man's tears.

"Javier, I don't know what to tell you. When Jade died I wasn't around."

"Yeah right, I should've known you would protect him."

"No, honestly. I don't know what I gotta do for you to believe that I have no loyalty to that dude anymore. Rich is a non-motherfucking factor and he can kiss my ass."

"Yeah right."

"You're acting like my so-called father is another dude I fucked behind your back. I wouldn't protect him. I need you to believe me."

"Aight, aight, movin' on. Do you think Jade was right to think Rich had somethin' to do wit' Carlos' death?" Javier asked.

"She was absolutely right. Rich killed my Uncle Carlos because he found out him and Lisa were fucking. Then they covered it up so Uncle Renzo wouldn't take everybody out."

To redeem myself and let Javier know he could trust me, I told him all that I knew about the Carlos situation. He was shocked at the way things went down and the details, but you could tell he was also shocked that I'd confirmed Jade's story. After selling my soul to my new man, we made love again. This time was better because it felt like it wasn't just sex.

"I want you to have my baby, Denie."

"Cum inside of me, baby," I whispered.

"Ahh- Ahh. Damn, Denie, Ahhhhh." Between my legs was filled with the liquid of love and it felt good.

As we laid in each other's arms, within minutes I'd dozed off to sleep until suddenly being awakened by some strange dude.

"J, what's up man, who dis?" the dark skinned guy questioned as he peered over at me like a piece of meat.

"Man, T-Roc, didn't I tell you to call me before you

came over here. This my girl, Denie," Javier responded.

"Damn, this the same chick you been chillin' wit' since you came back from D.C." The strange man looked at me again. "When you goin' back home, Ma? You movin' in or somethin'?"

"Excuse me? Last time I checked we don't know each other, so my business ain't your business," I snapped. "Javier, who the hell is this guy and how did he get in here?"

Ignoring me, Javier got out of bed naked to grab his sweatpants and put them on.

"Yo' come on man, time for you to give my girl some privacy. Let's go." Javier escorted T-Roc out of the bedroom before going downstairs.

His black-ass definitely creeped me out but, I had to act unfazed so he wouldn't think I was scared of him.

Getting out of bed, I slipped on one of Javier's wife beaters along with a pair of shorts I lounged around in, then went downstairs. I wanted to see what the hell they were up to. Once I realized Javier and T-Roc were in the guestroom with the music blazing, I tried to open the door, but it was locked.

"What the hell is going on?" I asked, knocking on the door.

After calling Javier's name and knocking a couple more times the door finally swung open. Both of their eyes were bright red as the strong weed odor escaped into the air. Up until now, I didn't even know Javier smoked.

"What bitch? Damn, we tryna handle bizness and you interruptin' us!" T-Roc yelled with an attitude.

"Who the fuck do you think you're talking to you bitch-ass nigga?" I yelled back.

Javier waved his arms like a referee. "Yo', yo' Denie, go the fuck back upstairs. I'll be up there in a minute."

"You betta check this nigga before I get his ass killed," I warned.

"Yo' bitch, you in Brooklyn. This ain't D.C. Bitches get stitches for sendin' death threats. I don't give a fuck who yo' pops is!" T-Roc said.

"Denie, go upstairs! T-Roc, fall back man," Javier tried to intervene.

Rolling my eyes, I went back upstairs pissed off. Nelson would've never allowed anyone to talk to me like that. I didn't understand why T-Roc had a problem with me when he didn't even know who I was. The more I laid in Javier's room waiting for him to come upstairs, the more I felt I'd made a huge mistake. I'd told him entirely too much.

Chapter 14

Lisa

As I looked around the media room I couldn't believe my eyes. Every one of these crazy muthafuckas was in unison, signing to the top of their lungs...coned birthday hats, snotty noses and all.

"Happy birthday to you, happy birthday to you, happy birthday dear Lisa, happy birthday to you. How old are you? How old are..."

"None of your fucking business!" I yelled then threw down the stupid Happy Birthday hat that one of the nurses had forced everyone to wear.

I wasn't turning three years old, and there was nothing happy about this fucking day. Suddenly, several of the patients started blowing their party horns like it was fucking New Year's Eve. They didn't seem the least bit phased by my outburst.

"Yeah!" the other patients cheered and clapped their hands.

They became even more hyped once they saw another nurse cutting the ugly-ass sheet cake the hospital had obviously bought from some grocery store. There had to be a way for me to get out of this Godforsaken place. These people really were crazy if they thought I belonged here.

How could Rich and my mother do this to me?

As I slid my chair back away from the table, Mary, an older white woman who's room was directly next to mine started talking. Ever since the first day I arrived, her breath always smelled like she'd just ate a bag some bad fish.

"Lisa, where are you going?" Mary asked.

"Mary, go play in traffic, damn."

"Why should I do that? I would get hit by a car or something."

"That's my point. Slow Sally."

"Lisa, you know I'm Mary."

Feeling an instant headache coming on, I placed my hand on my forehead. "Mary, please shut the fuck up!"

"It's your birthday. You should be happy."

"I won't ever be happy until I get away from you psycho muthafuckas!" I belted.

"Nurse, nurse, Lisa hurt my feelings," Mary cried like a five year old.

I couldn't believe the old bitch was actually crying real tears.

This place was insane, I thought before getting up from the table and strutting to my room.

This wasn't the way I wanted to bring in my first birthday divorced from Rich. I always envisioned me partying and getting laid at the end of the night by somebody I'd just met. I just wanted to do the unexpected, but my life had definitely taken a turn. God knows I wanted to get out of this hell hole and enjoy my birthday. Anywhere but here would do.

I wasn't even in my room ten minutes before someone knocked on the door.

"If that's one of them foolish-ass people trying to sing happy birthday again, it's gonna be a damn problem."

Opening the door with a serious attitude, I stared at Nurse Betty with an evil glare.

"What the hell do you want?"

"You have a gift from someone," she replied, with a nice sized box in her hand.

I snatched the package away from her. "Thank you. You can leave now."

"Lisa, you really should stop focusing on being so rude toward people and try to smile. You're going to overcome this. You're different from the others."

"Oh really? Well, if I'm so different why can't I have anymore visitors for a while?"

"Because you attacked your cousin that last time she was here," Nurse Betty advised.

"How many times do I have to tell y'all that bitch wasn't my fucking cousin? Besides, she attacked me!" I pointed to the small scar under my right eye.

"Lisa, there's no need to get upset. Maybe the Director will be willing to let you have visitors again once you prove that you're able to control your temper. I'm not here to decide who attacked who first. Be happy that you got your cell phone back. Most patients don't even have that privilege."

I wasn't in the mood for her lecture. "Are you done?"

Nurse Betty looked like she wanted to slap some sense into me. "Actually, I am," she said, before turning around and slamming my door.

Not giving a damn if she was mad or not, I inspected the box that had two cards attached along with a beautiful pink ribbon. I couldn't wait to see what was inside, and even more so who the sender was. Looking at how well the package was wrapped, I knew for sure that it wasn't from my mother because this definitely wasn't her style. Her cheap-ass only used dollar store gift bags with a little tissue paper stuffed inside. Looking at my calligraphy written name on the card, I knew the box had to be from Cornell.

Maybe he had a change of heart, I thought. Before I could open the envelope my phone rang, it was Jermaine.

"Hello, Jermaine."

"Happy Birthday, Boo-lite!"

"Thanks babe."

"Sista, do me a fava. Look in your room and please tell me that my work bag is still under the desk."

"Your bag?"

"Yes, Chile. I haven't seen it since I did your hair that day."

"Hold up, let me look. Is it a blue MCM tote?" I asked a few seconds later.

"Yes. Thank God. I was stressing because my good shears and razors are in there. Girl, I just got back from ATL and had a client this morning that I needed to give a razor cut and didn't have my tools. I was praying to God them people in that place didn't take my stuff after I had to sneak it in there."

"Well, it's still here."

"Alright, well, you know me not having my tools is messing with my coins, so I'll be up there later on today to pick it up and bring your birthday gift I brought you back from Atlanta."

"Thanks sweetheart. Now, let me get back to opening my birthday gifts?"

"Of course, Miss Thang. Love you."

"Love you more."

Opening the first envelope, I pulled out a card titled, *"From Your Son on Your Special Day."* Thinking that was rather odd, I stared at the word son for a few seconds, before a picture of Juan and I fell out.

"What the hell is going on?" I said to myself before reading the card.

Hoping every hour of your birthday brings you reasons to smile, and not a minute goes by without you knowing just how much you are loved. Wishing you a day that's as special as you are.

Love Forever,
Your Son
Juan

PS...Mom I'm okay. Don't worry we'll be together
soon, I promise.

I was confused. Was my son really alive? I needed more answers. My mind started running rapidly as I instantly got emotional. Juan was my world and to know that he was really alright overwhelmed me with anxiety. Not only did I miss him like crazy, I needed him now more than ever.

I gazed at his signature for a few moments, remembering the exact way he made the loop for his J. "Oh my God. I can't believe this."

As tears rolled down my face, I reached for the gift before opening the next card. I really had to know what was inside now. Tearing the beautiful paper off and opening up the box, I peeled off the several layers of black tissue paper before realizing there was nothing inside.

What the hell, I thought.

Just when I was about to turn the box over, I saw a red piece of tissue paper at the bottom that had something inside. Thinking this entire situation was bizarre, I grabbed the paper and opened it. When I saw my Tiffany barrette inside, I immediately felt sick to my stomach. I didn't know what to think.

Ripping the next envelope open by this point, the second card had a huge clown on the front. As soon as I opened it up, the card started singing, *Tears of a Clown* by Smokey Robinson.

Now there's some sad things known to man
But ain't too much sadder than...the tears of a clown
When there's no one around.

However, the picture of Denie and Cornell that was inside, literally had me fuming. There she was, hugged all up on him while both of them smiled from ear to ear. It even looked as if Cornell was enjoying her company from the way he leaned in. I was heated. My hands even began to shake as I opened the letter inside the card as well.

Hey Lisa,
Yes, I took the time out of my life to put this special birthday gift together for you. No, Juan isn't alive dummy. I

knew I would get you with that one. I forged his name really good don't you think? As I write this heartfelt birthday note, I'm sitting here cracking up laughing at how mad you must really be right now. Okay, so I know you're wondering what's up with me and Cornell. Well, I can see why you were loving him because he's a great guy and the sex is out of control. I heard those ball players could ball out in the bedroom, but damn girl why did you choose the coke over his fine ass. I get high off his love alone. Well, I don't want to get you all moist thinking about my new man, I just want to thank you for leading me to him. At first it was all about getting back at you, but now I really love him. He's just what I needed in my life. Now that Rich doesn't want you, Cornell is with me, and Juan is gone, you ain't got shit. That's why I thought it was important to be there for you at the lowest point in your life. Happy Birthday bitch. Oh, and have fun in the nut house.

> *Yours Truly,*
> *Denie*

The bitch had the audacity to kiss the letter with red lipstick. To say that I was furious would've been putting it lightly. The fact that she was sick enough to send me a card and sign Juan's name told me that her ass needed to be in this place and not me. When my thoughts suddenly shifted to Cornell, I picked up the phone and dialed his number immediately. The phone went to voicemail the first two times I called, but I hadn't planned on giving up. By the time I called a third time, he finally decided to answer.

"Didn't I tell you not to call my phone anymore!" he belted.

"Fuck you, Cornell! I thought you were different but all y'all niggas the same. How are you gonna go and fuck Denie!"

"Man, get off my phone Lisa! I don't owe you shit. You really do need help!"

He hung up on me, but I called his ass right back. I ended up calling at least six more times, but each of my calls were directed to his voicemail. I ended up leaving three hateful messages, until I heard a familiar voice. It was Juan.

"Ma, you should've listened to me. I told you not to fuck with him."

Looking up, I saw my son standing near the door. I hadn't even heard him come in. "Juan, is it really you? Is it really you, Juan?"

"Yes Ma, happy birthday." He moved closer to the bed.

Dropping my phone, I covered my mouth in complete disbelief. "Oh, my God, Juan. You're still alive." I stood up to hug him, but he held up his hand.

"Ma, you can't tell anybody. The Feds snuck me here to see you, so I don't have a lot of time."

"Oh my goodness, please just hear me out. I always wanted to tell you how sorry I was for arguing with you that day. I love you Juan and I hope that you can forgive me. Can you get me out of here? Juan, I need you to sign me out of here. Can you do that for me?"

"Ma, no one can know that I'm alive."

"But Juan I don't belong here. Do you think I'm crazy, too? All you have to do is take me out on a pass."

As I pleaded with my son, one of the white, younger nurse's, Gretchen walked in.

"Lisa, are you ready for your dinner?"

"Nurse Gretchen, this is my son Juan. He's taking me on a home pass today for my birthday. Juan tell her."

He seemed pissed that she'd seen him in there.

"Juan, it's okay, tell her. Tell her that you're taking me out to dinner for my birthday."

"Lisa, there's no one here. Your son passed away. Don't you remember?" Gretchen asked.

I pointed. "Gretchen, he's right there. Don't try to make it seem like I'm crazy."

"You're not crazy sweetie, but you are here alone," she assured.

When I turned back around, Juan was gone. I had no idea how he'd left the room without her seeing him. I also couldn't believe that he'd left me once again. No matter what Nurse Gretchen said, I knew for a fact that I'd seen my son. He was there.

"So, are having dinner in your room sweetheart? Or since it's your birthday do you wanna switch it up and eat in the media room?"

"No, and I'm not your fucking sweetheart!" I snapped.

She left out of the room shaking her head and no longer pressing the issue about me eating. I felt so alone and defeated. Not only had my son left me at a time when I needed him the most, but Cornell had made it clear that he didn't want anything to do with me as well. What the hell was wrong with me? Maybe Denie was right. I was worthless and no one wanted me. Even my mother hadn't been back to see me since our argument over a month ago. That bitch didn't have any problems staying up in my house, but couldn't even pick up the phone to call.

Was I being punished for killing my own daughter, I started to think.

If Carlie was here, maybe Cornell and I could've raised her together. Maybe she was my savior and I'd ruined it by taking her life.

Drowning in my sorrows, I suddenly felt like I didn't deserve to live anymore. Feeling completely alone, I laid across my bed and cried feeling sorry for myself. As the tears started to burn my eyes, all of a sudden something came over me. I got up and started pacing the room back and forth.

"I hate all of you!" I yelled. "Fuck everybody!"

My body seemed to be consumed with rage until I suddenly heard my father's voice.

Lisa come to me. Come to your Daddy. I love you. I'll always love you. Carlos is here with me and we'll both love you forever. Carlie is here, too. She forgives you. Come to us. No one here will ever hurt you. No more Rich. No more Denie. No more of your mother. She never really loved you or me anyway. Come with me my daughter. I'll love you for eternity.

That's when it clicked. I knew what I had to do and

didn't understand why it took me so long to figure it out. Instantly, I jumped up and went straight to Jermaine's work bag. All this time my ticket out of this place was right under my nose.

Walking over to the desk, I prepared for the meeting with my father. It was time to face everyone I'd ever let down. Since my father had promised me that Carlos and Carlie had forgiven me, I was ready to see them. We would all be a family. That's all I ever wanted. I just wanted to be loved. I'd been weak for Rich and everyone else for so long. Now, I wanted to be strong. I wanted to escape Rich and everyone else who'd caused me pain.

As I dumped the bag on the desk, I picked up the razor as a slight smile appeared on my face. There it was… my one way ticket home. It was finally time. I laid back on the bed and prepared myself. After saying a quick prayer I placed the razor to my throat.

"Here I come, Daddy," I said just before it was finally over.

Chapter 15

Marisol

"So, you decided to short me on my money, nigga? You think just because Renzo is locked up and I run shit now that you can just do whatever the fuck you want? You think just because I'm a female, you can't be dealt with?"

I knew I shouldn't have been talking so reckless over the phone, but my anger had obviously clouded my judgment.

"Marisol, I swear to you, I counted that shit five times. It was all there. I swear on my kids, I would never cheat you," Devin pleaded.

Instead of me responding, I hung up on his ass. Devin had been doing business with our family for over ten years and we'd never had issues with him in the past. In the real world, that might've stood for something, but in this game…no one could be trusted. I wasn't stupid. I'd placed every stack of cash in the money machine, and each time the amount came to ninety thousand. It was short by ten grand. When Renzo heard about this he was gonna be pissed.

"Devin gotta be involved with this shit," I said to myself. "Ten stacks aren't just gonna fucking disappear."

Retracing my steps, I remembered both Carmen and Maria being sound asleep when I got home from meeting Devin and Rich was on his way out. He'd been right by my side since Mia passed away. After he left, I threw the bag of money on the bed, then jumped in the shower. I didn't even start counting it until after I got out, and the bag hadn't been disturbed. I didn't know what was going on, but I wasn't gonna be the one to pay for this mishap.

The more I sat in my robe throwing the money through the counter one more time, the more I thought about my life. My heart really wasn't in this game anymore. However, no matter how much I struggled with getting out, I had so many of Renzo's lose ends to tie up, it wasn't gonna be that easy to just walk away, especially with Armondo being locked up, too. I wished I could just hand it all over to Rich and be done, but Renzo would never allow that. He still called questioning me about Carlos' death almost every fucking day. That man wasn't gonna rest until he found out who was responsible. A part of me wanted to tell him that Lisa was the one responsible so he could be at peace, but the plan was to let him know in due time. After I took care of her ass, then I would fill him in.

Glancing at the picture of Mia on the wall, I instantly got emotional. The memories of my daughter held both joy and pain. I remembered how colicky she was as an infant and I prayed for a full night's sleep. I remembered how her diapers always drooped when she first learned to walk. I remembered her first birthday when she stuck her face in the cake. I remembered when I had to leave her for the first time. I remembered her little body sleeping next to me sometimes and how much comfort I got with her near me. I remembered how much I loved her.

It all happened so fast, I was still in shock that she was gone. There wasn't a day that went by that I didn't think about my baby. There also wasn't a day when I didn't feel guilty about not spending enough time with her before she died. No matter how much I always said, 'I'm a mother first', my actions hadn't reflected that over the past few months, and I felt bad. I loved my kids and all I ever wanted to do was give them a better life than I had. I hated that bitch Lisa with a passion, but now I could actually sympathize with her when she lost Juan. This was the worst pain I'd ever felt in my life. Anyone who'd ever said, a mother should never have to bury their child was absolutely right. This type of agonizing grief was way too much to bear. The more I thought about Mia, the more I got worried about Denie and tried calling her again, only to get her voicemail.

Hi this is Denie. Leave me a message and I'll think about calling you back. Beep.

"Hey, Denie, it's your mother. I'm so worried about you. Please, all I'm asking for is to know that you're okay. I promise not to question you if that's not what you want. Listen, I know you think you know Javier, but it's not good that you're with him right now. Denie, he's using you to get to me and your father and I fear for your life. Please come home. Call me back."

At this point, I prayed that she was still alive. Since Javier knew in his heart that Rich had killed Jade, his plans were unknown. After dealing with Mia's death, I hadn't even had the energy to try and look for Denie, but I guess that's what it was gonna boil down to if she didn't eventually call us back. Surprisingly, Rich seemed to think that Denie was just being rebellious, but something told me it was much deeper than that.

Staring back at Mia's portrait, I removed it from the wall before turning the dial to my safe. After placing the bag of money inside, I closed the door and put the picture back. Rich was standing in the doorway when I turned around, which scared the living shit out of me.

"Boy! You scared me. Why didn't you say something?"

"Because I enjoy lookin' at your ass?"

I wasn't in the mood to flirt, but let some of my frustrations out instead. "I feel so damn overwhelmed right now." Tears immediately started to flow.

"Awww, come here."

As Rich held me, it felt so good to have him comfort me without sex. Our relationship had basically been built off of a one night stand, so I rarely got this side of him.

"This business is taking a toll on me. I don't need the money. I just want to be a mother again. My life has always revolved around this business, so I'm at a point where I want out. I have no idea where Denie is and Mia is gone. I just feel like my life is spiraling out of control."

"Well, if you want I can take care of the business and you can focus on the kids."

"You know Lorenzo wouldn't be happy about that. With Juan and the whole Feds thing, the business partners in Columbia and L.A. don't want to do business with you. They don't even know I still really have dealings with you."

"So, what are you sayin'?"

"I'm saying they don't wanna fuck with you, Rich."

"Do you?" he questioned in a defensive tone.

"You're here aren't you? Don't question my loyalty. Don't forget how you betrayed me by covering up what Lisa did."

"You left my daughter on my doorstep and now she hates me because of you."

I shook my head. "Ah-ha, I knew it. That's what I thought. You still blame me."

"It is what it is. She hates me because I tried to protect her and have Lisa act as her mother."

"My husband is dead because of that stupid bitch, who's on borrowed time by the way. As soon as I find Denie, she's next on my checklist."

"I hate her, too, but Los is the reason why she got caught up on drugs. He chose to fuck her."

"And you chose to fuck me. You might not be breathing right now if it wasn't for me moving back to Puerto Rico and hiding my pregnancy."

"Come on now Marisol, do you really think that me and Los would beef over you, especially back then? It was always money over bitches wit' us. We've fucked tons of the same bitches. I didn't kill Los over Lisa…"

"What did you just say?" I asked cutting him off.

"Me and Los never beefed over nobody and he would still be here if it wasn't for a bitch."

"No, hold up. You just said that you killed Carlos!"

Rich's eyebrows wrinkled. "No the fuck I didn't. You trippin'."

"Don't sit here and play stupid. I know what the fuck I heard."

"Man, I ain't got time for this bullshit."

Before Rich could leave out the room, his phone rang. Taking it from his clip, his eyes increased tremendously only a few seconds after saying hello. Sitting on the edge of the bed, Rich ran his hand over his face just before hanging up.

"Lisa committed suicide today."

Hell, I was shocked myself. "Are you serious?"

"Yeah, that was the Director at the hospital. The found her body about an hour ago. She cut her throat with a razor."

"Damn, that bitch beat me to the punch."

I couldn't believe Rich had the nerve to look at me like my last comment was foul. I threw my hands in the air.

"What? Why you acting like I didn't have any plans to take that bitch out. I wanted her ass to have a miserable death for what she did to Carlos," I said. "Oh well, now I guess that's one less body I gotta ask God to forgive me for."

Again, Rich looked at me strangely. "Wow. I gotta go."

"So, you about to shed a tear for that bitch?" When Rich didn't reply, I became even more enraged. "Well, if that's the case maybe you do need to leave. I can't believe your daughter is missing and instead of you being concerned about that you're over here acting like some weak-ass dude." The bitch was definitely coming out.

"Marisol, fuck you!"

"Fuck you. I don't need no bitch-ass niggas around me."

When he started inching closer toward me I knew I'd struck a nerve.

"What you gonna do, hit me? I ain't Lisa. If you put your

hands on me, you leaving in a body bag, nigga."

Rich let out a slight chuckle. "I'm out."

Watching him storm out, I didn't give a damn if Lisa was his ex-wife or not. That bitch deserved to die after all the shit she'd done. Hell, she'd done me a favor by killing herself. Now, I didn't have to get my hands dirty.

"I really wanna know if her ass is really gone though," I said. "I need to hear that shit for myself."

Grabbing my cell phone, I quickly dialed the hospital's number.

"Thanks for calling Saint. Elizabeth's, how may I direct your call?" a woman asked.

"Yes, can you please transfer me to room 115?"

"Room 115 is no longer being occupied. May I ask whom I'm speaking with?"

"Marisol Sanchez. Lisa Sanchez is my sister-in-law. That was the last room I visited her in. I'm sorry, was her room changed?"

The woman paused for a few seconds. "I'm sorry Mrs. Sanchez, but Lisa passed earlier today. I thought someone notified her family already."

I let out a slight whimper. "Oh my goodness. I can't believe this."

"Again, I'm so sorry that you had to find out this way, Mrs. Sanchez," the woman spoke.

I began to sniff like I was crying. "Thanks for letting me know."

Now with Lisa now off my list, I could concentrate on Rich. That muthafucka had lost his mind if he thought he was gonna play me. I knew damn well I'd heard him say that he killed Carlos. I needed to get down to the bottom of this situation and knew just the person to get me the answers I needed.

Chapter 16

Rich

"Ahh shit! Ahh shit," I said, pullin' away from Lisa's funeral.

Even though she looked so peaceful in the ugly-ass walnut coffin her mother picked out, I was glad that bitch was finally gone. Now, it was time for me to collect and I couldn't have been happier. All the money I'd invested into Lisa over the years, who would've ever thought that her death would be the reason I got back on my feet. I hated playin' the mournin' ex-husband role all week, but it was going to be worth it once the check from her life insurance came.

When she first died, I was a little nervous that my payout wouldn't be approved since her dumb-ass had committed suicide. However, after lookin' over the paperwork from Lisa's house, luckily the suicide clause in the policy was only for the first two years. Since we'd gotten that policy almost fifteen years ago, none of that suicide clause shit mattered anymore. I was about to be a wealthy man again, and it felt good. I even had my lawyer tryin' to overturn all of Lisa's assets back to me.

She'd been so fucked up in the head after we got divorced, I'm sure my name was still on the majority of the shit anyway.

"Damn, I still can't believe Marisol fell for that shit. She really thought I was upset about Lisa killin' herself," I said like someone was listenin'

Why would I get upset about somethin' like that when Lisa had done me a favor, too? I'd stayed up countless nights tryin' to think of a way to kill Lisa and get my money, so I considered this a blessin'. The only thing I was upset about was the way I'd slipped up and said I killed Los. Now, that shit was stupid.

How could I be so damn careless?

Tryin' to focus on somethin' else, as soon as I was far enough away from Harmony Cemetery, I threw my tie in the backseat, then put my Jay-Z CD on blast. I was ready to be back on my boss shit.

The motivation for me, is them telling me what I could not be, oh well, Pharrell sang on the hook.

I was back and it felt good. Wit' my paper about to get a major upgrade, who knows, maybe I would give all this street shit up and go legit. Maybe buy a smallt apartment buildin' in D.C.or somethin'. I could've seen myself as a landlord. Damn, my man Jay had me feelin' motivated as shit off his Blueprint 3 CD. It was time for me to claim back everything I'd worked hard for startin' wit' my house. I decided to drive to my old residence the long way so I could enjoy the scenery and get my mind right. There was no need for Marisol or Trixie unless they were servin' me in bed. It was time for me to get mine. I was determined to land back on top, and if I had to get Marisol out of the way to make that happen, so be it.

When I pulled up to the house almost thirty minutes later, there were a bunch of cars leadin' up to the house. Wonderin' what the fuck First Lady was up to, I hopped out of the car and made my way up to the front door. As soon as I walked inside, there were people all over my place. Most had plates in their hands, so I knew it must've been Lisa's repass goin' on, but I didn't care. I thought everyone was gonna go back to Lisa's father's church for that shit. Why come here to eat somebody's nasty collard greens, fried chicken and hard-ass bread? I was pissed.

"What the fuck are all y'all doin' in my house?"

Within seconds, First Lady shot around the corner wit' her huge black hat still in place. "I beg your pardon, Rich."

"You heard me. Why the hell are all these people here? I didn't approve this."

From all the stares she got, I'm sure First Lady was embarrassed.

"I didn't need your approval. We're mourning my daughter's death, so please respect all these people and Lisa's home," she scolded.

"This ain't Lisa's home anymore This my shit and I want all of y'all to get the fuck out. I could barely get in the driveway because of all those damn cars outside!"

Everybody was takin' me for a joke, so I had to go to extreme measures to show them I wasn't bullshittin'. Not that I really had a pistol on me, but I did some fake shit just to scare Lisa's timid-ass family.

Puttin' my hand under my Armani suit like I was about to pull out a gun, I yelled, "Am I gonna have to lay all y'all down in here? How many times I gotta tell y'all to get the fuck out my shit!"

At that moment, people started runnin' out of the house so fast, you would've thought I was one of them Arab muthafuckas wit' a bomb strapped to my chest. The only one left standin' of course was, First Lady. She was all of 5'0 and obviously the toughest one out of the bunch.

She stood wit' her hands on her small hips in complete disbelief. "You're Satan himself. I just buried my daughter and can't believe even a gutter nigga like yourself would disrespect her like this."

I flashed a quick smile. "Damn, First Lady, I didn't know you had all that sin up in you. I struck a nerve, huh?"

"You're going straight to hell and if I have anything to do with it, you will pay!" she roared. "And I know you were the one who took my credit card. You had to take it that day you broke in. If the credit card people ask me to prosecute, I'm gonna say, yes!"

"You think I really give a fuck about anything you sayin' right now? All that shit sounds foreign. Ain't nobody take your damn credit card. I got my own loot. You know what…time for you to go, too."

Grabbin' the sleeve of her black knit St. John's dress, I pulled her ass toward the front door until she snatched her arm away.

"Get your hands off of me. I'm not going anywhere. This is my daughter's house! You're no longer married, so you're not entitled to anything in this house. If anything, Denie is her only child and this would all be hers."

I had to laugh. "You're dumber than I thought. If you noticed, Denie wasn't at the funeral today, and it's a reason for that. Denie isn't Lisa's child. That's Marisol's daughter. I was fuckin' both of them and your dumb-ass daughter did what she was told. She raised Denie as her own."

"You're a liar," First Lady said in disbelief.

"If I've never told your old-ass the truth about nothin' else, I'm tellin' you the truth right now. Lisa doesn't have any more kids. All of her assets are gonna be given back to me as well as a hefty insurance policy."

"You're so evil! I've always hated you. I hate that my daughter ever met you. I blame you for her death!"

"Well, if you hate me so bad then get the fuck out of my house." I walked over to the door and opened it.

"You can't just put me out!" she screamed.

"Watch me."

"Juan Sanchez, you're going to get yours. Karma is a bitch!"

"No, you're a bitch! Whatever you got in here, I'll have that shit shipped."

After slammin' the door, I immediately felt a weight lifted. Finally, I could have a piece of mind in my own house without a bitch naggin' me, and that shit felt good. All I needed to do was call ADT to change the code on the alarm just in case First Lady took me for a joke, and everything would be all good. Walkin' back into the kitchen, I noticed there were plates of food everywhere. It was definitely a must that I got Maria over here quick to get this shit cleaned up.

As I walked back toward the foyer and made my way upstairs, I began to think about what I was gonna do for an occupation once again. Now, it was gonna take longer than usual for me to get back on top because very few people were fuckin' wit' me once they found out that Juan was a snitch. I'm sure everyone thought The Feds were gonna be on my back more than ever, which I had to agree wit'. It was still hard to believe how my boy had fucked up what me and Los worked so hard to build in the streets. Now, I really had to make some decisions about goin' legit. Until then, I had to continue peelin' away at Marisol's bread every chance I got and stack until my check came

Marisol trusted me so much that she didn't realize that I knew the code to her safe and took ten to fifteen thousand from her on a regular. She never suspected me. I'm sure she didn't even think twice about me takin' the last ten thousand from her when she came back from meetin' Devin. I was good at what I did, and didn't feel the least bit remorseful. Besides, Marisol owed me anyway for lyin' all these years.

Cuttin' my thoughts about how weak Marisol could be at times, it dawned on me that I'd promised Juanita I was comin' to see her after the funeral. The last thing I wanted to do was disappoint my baby. She was all I had left since Denie wasn't fuckin' wit' me anymore. Since Denie wanted to act grown, I'd made up my mind not to press her out anymore. Ignornin' me and Marisol's calls was an ultimate sign of disrespect, so Denie was just gonna have to find out about that snake, Javier, on her own. Not that I wished anything bad on my daughter. I just gave

Javier enough benefit of the doubt. No matter if me and Denie were beefin' or not, his ass would die if he ever thought about hurtin' her. She was still my blood.

My phone suddenly rung, interruptin' my deep thoughts. It was my connect in Houston who was one of the most loyal dudes I fucked wit' in this business.

"Wassup, Grady?"

"What up, Rich?"

"Chillin'. I ain't got nothin' for you though."

"Naw, I was actually callin' to get Marisol's number from you."

I was caught off guard. "For what?"

"Well, since you chillin' I thought I'd holler at her."

I was a little irritated that Marisol was eatin' off the connect I'd established and wasn't breakin' me off wit' some money. That was one of the main reasons why I didn't give a fuck about peelin' from her ass. It was a perfect example of why she shouldn't be runnin' this empire. She was too weak. If I was able to take from her so easily and go unnoticed, somebody else could do the same. Shit, without all that I'd laid down in this game, Marisol wouldn't have all that shit now. Then it dawned on me. There was no way I was gonna let Grady slip out of my hands.

"How about you come up here and we meet. I'll make sure you good. I'll talk to her for you. She's been real cautious lately, but since you good peeps I'll make sure she look out."

"I'm already in town. You got time to holler at me today? I need to handle business ASAP. I got people waitin' on me."

"Alright, that's cool. Meet me out Clinton at that spot we used to get drinks at."

"Bet. I'll be there in a half hour."

"Make it a hour and a half, cuz I'm in the city and I gotta go to another spot to change my clothes and shit."

"Cool."

Grady couldn't have picked a more perfect time to call. I knew I could overcharge him because of the shortage goin' on right now. Nobody could get a good deal on coke these days. I also knew that I could take some shit from Marisol and she would never know. Keepin' her supply in Carlos' old stash spot had been the perfect suggestion. She was so easy to influence, it was quite pathetic.

****

Business wit' Grady was always smooth and to the point. After makin' a quick fifty g's, I made my way toward Trixie's house. She'd already called me to death wonderin' where I was. I knew she was gonna ask me for some money which is another reason why I decided to handle that Grady situation first. I just had to warn that nigga not to run his mouth to Marisol so I could keep him in my back pocket for when I needed some extra bread.

As soon as I walked in Trixie's house thirty minutes later, she immediately started runnin' her fuckin' mouth.

"What took you so long to get over here? You said you were in Clinton almost two hours ago."

"Girl, shut up! I'm here, ain't I?"

Trixie looked good as shit and the more she poked her lips out with an attitude I could see that red lipstick smeared all over my dick.

"You still fucking Marisol, ain't you?" she nagged.

"Man, stop worryin' about the next bitch. If you want us to fuck wit' each other, you need to stop trippin' all the damn time."

"Well, I know how to put it down in the bedroom, so you shouldn't have a need to go anywhere else."

"Whatever, I don't feel like this shit right now."

"You never do," Trixie said wit' an attitude as she followed me upstairs to Juanita's room.

My daughter was sleeping so peacefully.

"You need to lower your voice before you wake her up," I warned.

"Oh, now you so concerned about her."

"Look, if you keep talkin' shit I'ma roll out," I threatened.

"That's all you ever do, Rich! All I ever wanted for you to do is love me. No matter what, I've never been enough. Not for you or anyone else."

"What do you mean anybody else? You talkin' 'bout that loser- ass nigga, Mike?" I wanted her to bring that nigga's name up so I could backhand her ass.

"No! I'm just getting older and I want to be settled."

I burst out laughin'. "Who the fuck was gonna wife your freak-ass, Trixie?"

"Why do you have to be such a fucking asshole? Here I am pouring my heart out and all you can do is laugh?"

"Cuz that shit was funny. Trix, you've fucked damn near the whole DMV, who's gonna want to call you homebase wit' that kind of track record?"

By now it looked like steam was comin' out of her head. "Only God can judge me, Rich. If I'm such a whore, then why are you here? I'm the mother of your child?"

"By fault."

"No disrespect, but look at how your precious Lisa turned out. She was the perfect wife huh? God rest her soul."

Trixie took her index finger and motioned a cross. Little did she know I didn't give a fuck about either one of them.

"Fuck Lisa, and fuck you, too."

Trixie punched me in the arm. "So, that's all I'm good for is a fuck? You know what, all men are the same. You ain't no better than my father or any other man that has crossed my path. I don't know why I thought things would someday be different between us," she expressed in a sincere tone.

"Well, here's some advice for you. Don't ever put trust in any man. We ain't shit." I said then let out another big laugh.

Makin' my way back upstairs, I went to the kitchen to get me some water. Instead of hearin' Trixie constantly bitch, I would've rather had some of her A+ head action. It could've been the finishin' touch I needed to put me to sleep. Thinkin' I would suggest that, I ran back upstairs and headed to her bedroom. However, instead of findin' her naked, Trixie's ass was layin' on the floor in tears wit' a half finished a bottle of Rose' Moet by her side. I should've known that bitch had been drinkin' before I got there because she was talkin' way more shit than usual.

"Damn, you know how to make a nigga dick go soft. What the hell is wrong wit' you now?" I questioned.

"Rich, I'm tired of being judged, nobody will ever understand my struggles."

"Are you drunk?"

"No, I'm not drunk. I'm tired. Tired of men using me for my body, tired of being let down, and furthermore, tired of your ass."

"Well, I can leave."

"And run to Marisol. Is that who takes care of you when you get tired of me?"

I was so tired of Trixie whinin', I had to think of something to throw her off. "How do you think I could sleep with that bitch after what she did to me wit' Denie?"

"Is there someone else?"

"Man, stop questionin' me. What's goin' on wit' you, Trix? You gettin' all sentimental on me and shit."

"Our whole relationship…that's what's wrong. I was always second to Lisa. Now that she's out the picture, I want you to myself."

"You got me, now get over here and bounce on daddy's lap," I joked.

"Rich, I'm serious. All my life I've never had a man who truly loved me for me. And underneath all that you got going on, I thought you really cared about me."

As I listened to her cry and nag I started takin' my clothes off to prepare for the head she was about to give me. Little did she know I wasn't leavin' without it. I didn't wanna hear that shit she was talkin'. I just wanted to fuck, but I played nice to get what I wanted.

"I do care. But I also care about my need for you to come over here and give me some of that hot pocket."

"Listen to me, Rich, damn! This is the one time I have the courage to express the way I feel, so I need you to just listen to me."

"I'm all ears, wassup?" I asked in an annoyed tone.

As sexy as Trixie looked I had to have her, so if it meant I had to be her shrink to get some ass, I was down.

"From the time I was five until I was twelve, I was molested by some of the men in my family."

"Hold up, what?" My sexual mood instantly went out the window because I wasn't expectin' her to say something like that.

"It started with my mother's boyfriend, Smitty, for a couple of years. No matter how much I cried when she would leave me home with him, she never thought twice that it was a reason behind those tears. While she went out on the town cheating on Smitty, his payback was having his way with me and my older brother."

"Damn, so that's why he a fag. That's fucked up!"

"My brother is not a fag. He's a gay man who I love dearly. My mother wasn't a maternal person. All she cared about was her dudes and her drinks. She was an alcoholic and her drinking took her life around the time when I met you."

"So, the apple ain't fall far from the tree, huh?"

Trixie punched me again. "Damn Rich! You're such an asshole."

"Naw, I'm serious. I'm not tryin' to be funny. You were doin' what you saw your moms doin'. That's why I tell you all the time that you can't be havin' dudes around my daughter like that. I don't want her growin' up wit' your bad habits. Did your mother know what that dude did to y'all?"

"She tried to act like she didn't know at first, but when I was twelve she caught me sucking his dick. He used to make me go down on him when I was on my period. Of course she blamed me and that's how I ended up at my grandmother's house. She didn't want to accept the fact that he was molesting us. As long as he paid the bills, that's all she cared about."

After listenin' to Trixie's childhood it made me look at her totally different. Now, I understood why she was such a whore. After that drainin' conversation I had no desire for sex. She'd hit a nerve. I didn't condone anybody fuckin' an innocent child and I felt sorry for her. When she asked me to hold her, I didn't think that was askin' for too much. I guess she could suck me off in the mornin' after all the tears cleared up.

Chapter 17

The bitch finally kicked the bucket, I thought to myself as I re-read the mediatakeout.com story and bookmarked it in my I-Phone.

The headline read, *NBA Star Dumps Girlfriend and She Commits Suicide.* Little did they know, it was all me, not Cornell who'd sent Lisa over the edge. That deranged bitch didn't deserve to live after all she'd done to me, so I was beyond ecstatic. Life was finally going good.

Not only was I happy about Lisa's demise, but I was also pleased with the way my relationship with Javier's relationship was going. We'd been together for exactly seven weeks now, but the way I felt about him made it seemed like years. Being with him made me really look forward to living in New York permanently. Everything happened for a reason. It was fate that we'd hooked up. He made me feel like I mattered, and that's what I loved about him the most.

The only time we had issues was when his fucking friend, T-Roc, was around. That nigga made me sick. Not only did he have a lack of respect for women, but he acted like Javier owed him something. He also seemed jealous of our relationship and needed to find a girl of his own. Tonight Javier and I were finally having a night to ourselves out on the town and I was looking forward to it. Javier had started to dabble in the music industry and one of the execs was having an exclusive release party for one of the artists. Finally, he was leaving his entourage at home.

My cell phone started ringing with my baby's ringtone *Love All Over Me* by Monica.

"*I got love all over me, baby you touch every part of me…*" I started singing to the phone before answering.

"Hey baby!" I said with a big smile.

"What's my girl doin'?"

"Just got out of the shower, just got finished playing with my love box, and just can't wait for you to get home," I replied in a seductive tone.

"Word. Well, I had to drop somethin' off to T-Roc, but I'm about to leave here now. Start gettin' ready cuz I know how long that makeup shit be takin'."

"What should I wear?"

"I'll bring home the outfit that I picked up for you. It's a Black and White Diamond theme. The guys have to wear black with diamonds, and the girls have to wear white with diamonds."

"Ooh, sounds good. Can't wait to see what you bought me."

"Don't worry, I hooked you up. Now, get yourself together so all you have to do is slip on yo' clothes. I don't wanna be late."

"So, I guess that means no to a quickie, huh."

"Baby, we don't have time."

"We can do it while you're in the shower."

"I'm already dressed. I took a shower over here and got dressed so we wouldn't be late."

"Damn, Javier. I missed you. You've been gone all day

and I…"

"Denie, stop whinin' and shit. I'm on my way."

The phone went dead after T-Roc started complaining in the background about how Javier was acting like a bitch by explaining himself to me.

"He needs to mind his fucking business," I said, storming into the bathroom.

When Javier came home twenty minutes later and I saw the Bergdorf bags I knew he'd picked out nothing but the best. Unzipping the garment bag, I unveiled a beautiful white bandage dress by Herve Leger and these banging blinged out YSL Tribute pumps to match.

"This dress is gorgeous. I love it!" I exclaimed.

"Go ahead and put it on."

As I shimmied into the dress, which fit like a glove, Javier placed the shoes on my feet like I was Cinderella. I ran to the mirror like I was eight years old and got a flashback of my childhood when things were good and I used to play in Lisa's closet. I quickly snapped back to reality when Javier placed this beautiful diamond cross around my neck. I knew he had money, but this necklace looked like it cost a pretty penny. It had to have been well over five carats, and looked even better than the one Marisol wore.

"Oh my God, babe, this is beautiful."

Javier beamed. "Not as beautiful as you. Here are some more trinkets for you to doll up in. Tonight is important and could be what I need to go all the way legit. I have to impress these people."

As I opened the box, there was an oversized diamond flower ring and six diamond bangles. I felt like a million bucks. He really knew how to make a girl feel special. I never wanted for anything growing up, but it was a different feeling when you got gifts from someone you're in love with.

When we got to the garage, I wondered which car he would be driving and just like I thought, it was his snow white Maserati GranTurismo. With Javier dressed in an all black custom outfit, and a long, iced out diamond necklace, we looked just like money. He was so fit and trim that it was hard to believe that he weighed well over two-hundred and fifty pounds at one point. He told me that most of the men in his family were overweight, so he'd made a conscious effort to lose several pounds. I applauded him for taking control of his health, because the plus size dude in the picture over his fireplace would've never got the time of day with me, no offense.

When we pulled up to the star studded event in downtown Manhattan and hit the red carpet, cameras started flashing left and right. "Who are you wearing," was the question of the night. Thank God I was in to fashion because if I would've pronounced my designers name wrong, Javier would've been so embarrassed. This night was important to my man, so I wanted to make sure I didn't ruin it for him. I felt so special playing wifey.

Once we got inside, security ushered us to the VIP balcony that was for the elite only. There were so many groupies trying to make their way through the rope, I could've swatted them away like flies at a picnic.

"Naomi...Naomi!" someone called out.

I couldn't believe someone was calling out my alias. It was Cornell Willis. Javier immediately frowned when he came over to say hello. By it being so crowded Cornell couldn't tell Javier and I were together as we made our way to our table.

"What's up young lady? I'm still waiting for my dinner date," Cornell said. "Oh, my bad, I didn't know you were here with somebody," Cornell added, once Javier placed his hand around my waist to show I was taken.

"Damn, Denie, didn't he used to fuck wit' Lisa," Javier stated.

"Denie, huh? I thought your name was Naomi?" Cornell asked. He looked confused.

"Look, this is my man and I don't believe I know you. Come on babe let's go," I said, trying to dodge the bullet. I didn't want Javier to think I was some type of groupie.

We hadn't even gotten two feet away before Javier pulled me toward him.

"So, what's up wit' you and that nigga Cornell, Denie?"

"What? I don't know him like that."

"Why you lyin'? You told me that yo' name was Naomi at first. Did you forgot about that shit?"

I did forget, but there was no way I was gonna get caught up like that.

"Babe, he tried to talk to me one time and I wasn't having it because I knew he was fucking with Lisa. Yes, I told him my name was Naomi, but when I found out who he was the shit never went any further. Trust me, we never fucked around and that's all that matters. Let's enjoy our night. It's really not worth us ruining our evening."

Javier stared at me for a few moments, then finally softened his stance. "You're right sweetheart." He gave me kiss on the cheek, but somehow I had a feeling that this conversation wasn't over.

An hour later, the music was blazing and the bottles were popping all over the place. I made small talk with the ladies that were at our table while Javier handled business in between getting his drink on and partying. We were having such a good time. My glass didn't stay empty for two seconds before it kept getting filled back up. One of the executives' wives named Chasity was more my speed. She was a cute girl and young like me, so every time a down south rap song came on, we would stand up and start dancing with each other. We were both drunk, but she was being a little friskier than I wanted. I wasn't down with the girl thing, so I kept backing up. I shot Javier a look, but couldn't read his facial expression. He either enjoyed the view, or was trying to play it off to get on the music execs good graces.

"You having a good time?" Chasity asked, getting a little closer to me.

"Yes, but I'm drunk as hell."

"Me too. What are y'all doing later?"

"Girl, we're going home. Javier ain't the type to hang out."

"Well, if you want, y'all are welcome to come over to our house. We have a mansion right over in Alpine, New Jersey with lots of rooms."

"Oh, well umm…let me talk to Javier and I'll let you know."

"Put my number in your phone, and call me when y'all get to the car to let me know what's up," Chasity added.

"Okay."

I grabbed my phone and put her number in with no intentions on calling her. She must've thought just because I was being friendly with her that I was willing to share my man. I knew what that meant. Chasity and her husband must've been swingers. For the rest of the night as Javier handled business, I saw Chasity's husband, Blake, looking at me like I was a medium rare steak. This was probably something they did on a regular basis, but they weren't about to get me caught up.

Once the party was over and I got up to leave, my legs immediately collapsed. I was done. Javier even had to carry me to the valet because I was so twisted. He tried to play it cool, but I knew he was embarrassed. Javier barely said a word to me while we waited for our car, but once the car came and we pulled off, all hell broke loose.

"Yo', what the hell was that about? What, are you gay or somethin'?" Javier asked.

"Don't you dare go there with me after I just humiliated myself. You lucky I didn't smack the shit out of that girl and shut that entire VIP section down. That was your boy's wife. She was coming on to me!"

"Well, from where I was sittin' it looked like your drunk-ass liked it."

"I may be drunk, but I'm not gay. Your friends are the fucking swingers. Why did they think it was okay to come at me like that?"

"Look at how you were dancin' on the chick, Denie,"

Javier responded.

"I was just having fun. All I was trying to do was fit in with your friends while you talked about your business venture. Is that a crime? I was trying to have my man's back, but I see that you don't appreciate that shit!"

Our argument lasted until we got home, but eventually I started to feel bad because my words were beginning to sting. I knew that if I didn't shut up, Javier would send my ass back to D.C. so I tried to play nice. I even tried to get him to forgive me once we walked inside the loft, but Javier wasn't having it. He just ignored me.

"Please don't give me the silent treatment, baby. I'm sorry," I pleaded.

"Denie, go sleep that alcohol off," Javier finally said. He threw his car key down, then went to take off his shoes.

"But I'm not drunk anymore. I'm not even tipsy. I just want to make love to my man." When I walked up to him and tried to kiss his lips, he turned away.

"I'm good, Denie."

"I'm sorry, Javier. What do you want from me?"

"The truth. I'm startin' to wonder what type of chick you really are. First the NBA nigga was all in yo' face, then you start bumpin' and grindin' wit' Blake's wife. Who are you? Tell me the truth, have you ever been wit' a girl before?"

I was offended. "Hell no."

"You ever had a ménage a trois?"

"No," I said shaking my head.

"Would you have one if I asked you to?"

My eyebrows wrinkled. "What?"

"You heard me. Would you have a threesome if I asked you to?" Javier questioned again.

"Is that what it's gonna take for you to trust me and love me again?"

"I'm not gonna stop lovin' you just like that. But seriously would you do that for me?"

I paused for a few seconds. I needed him to trust me. "I

would do anything to make you happy."

"You promise?"

"I promise."

Deep inside I prayed that I wouldn't have to make good on that agreement.

Chapter 18

Tonight was the night I dreaded since I told Javier two weeks ago that I would do anything to make him happy. Keeping my word I'd agreed to a ménage a trois. Even though I was a pleaser in the bedroom, I'd never experienced three people in bed at one time, so I was nervous as hell. It was gonna take a whole lot of drinks and a couple of E pills to get me through this sexual experience. However, despite my apprehension, there was no turning back now. It was all or nothing.

Going to a boutique called The Pleasure Chest earlier that day, I left out the kinky store with three shopping bags and five hundred dollars worth of candles, lingerie, vibrators, lubricate and several other toys to assist in our eventful night.

After my day in the city, I relaxed by soaking in the Jacuzzi and sipped a glass of Reisling to get my mind right. I couldn't help but wonder who the mystery chick was going to be. Was it Chasity, or some bitch he was fucking with behind my back? My mind was all over the place when my phone rung a few minutes later. It was Javier.

"Hello."

"Hey, babe. You ready for tonight?"

"As ready as I'm going to be," I responded in a dry tone.

"What's wrong? Are you havin' second thoughts?"

I didn't want him to be disappointed, so my first instinct was to lie. "No, but I'm definitely gonna need an E pill or something. I'm not good with sharing, so seeing you with someone else is gonna fuck with me."

"All you need to know is that I belong to you."

"I know, but all this is new for me."

"Well, when it's too much for you just let me know and we can stop, okay?" He sounded so sincere.

I let out a huge sigh. "Alright."

"We'll be there around 10."

"Babe, it's 9:15."

"I know, so get ready because I'm ready to be inside of you. I want you to have the candles lit, and I also want you blindfolded. You cool wit' that?"

"Yeah."

"You know where the E at right?" Javier inquired.

"Yes."

"Cool. See you in a little bit," he said, then hung up.

"Love you, too," I said, putting my phone down.

Getting out of the water, I dried myself off before putting on some of my Almond Cookie Body Lotion by Carol's Daughter. I then removed my hot rollers that gave me big, sexy hair and sprayed on some body glitter. After deciding on a sexy, red thong set, I swallowed the Ecstasy along with three shots of Ciroc, and took a huge deep breath. It was almost showtime.

★★★★★★★★★★★★★★

"Baby, I'm home!" Javier yelled forty minutes later. "We got company. You ready?"

He always knew how to make me feel better. By the sound of his voice, he obviously wanted me to be comfortable and I loved him for that.

"Yeah!" I yelled back.

I'd set the mood with all the candles and rose petals leading to the bedroom, so you could tell Javier was impressed.

"Damn, baby you really did it up," he said, looking around the room. He then looked at me. "Wow, I don't know if I can share you lookin' all good like that."

"Can I take off the blindfold now?"

"No, not yet."

"Well, are you gonna tell me who you brought home?" I questioned. The suspense was killing me.

"Just lay back and enjoy our night. No more questions."

He started to kiss me on my neck first and as he worked his way down my body the flood gates opened. I was so wet. Maybe it was the drinks or the E pills, or maybe it was just the anticipation of me wanting this night to be over with all at the same time. Javier's soft kisses were tender as he worked my thong off with his teeth. Next, he sucked my toes, which instantly turned me on, but I couldn't help but wonder if my silver mirrored minx toenails would still be intact when he was done. As Javier worked his way back up my leg, he got lost in my pussy and flicked his tongue against my clit with just enough pressure that made me want to just cum all in his mouth. As he slurped and sucked my juices, I moaned wanting more.

"You like that baby?"

"I love it. I love you, Javier. I love you."

"I love you, too," he replied.

"Make love to me baby."

"We'll get to that."

After Javier used the furry handcuffs I'd bought to restrain me to the bed, something told me that the girl was up next. As I prepared for her soft gentle touch, all of a sudden things got rough. Instead of the girl making her move, Javier shoved his dick inside of me with a forceful thrust, which wasn't his style.

"Ouch, baby that hurts," I said. It felt like my pussy was

on fire as he continued to fuck me at a rapid pace. "Javier, you're hurting me!" I wailed.

At the moment, I started to wonder if this was a good idea. *Is he that fucking excited*, I thought to myself.

When Javier didn't respond, I tried to take it and act as if I was enjoying myself, but couldn't. The shit was hurting way too bad.

"Turn over," he said in a demanding tone.

Even though it was hard for me to maneuver with the handcuffs on, I was able to turn my body onto my stomach. Once I placed myself in the doggy position, he didn't waste time entering me from behind. Then all of a sudden I felt a tongue flicker across my clit again. Realizing that the girl had finally decided to join the party, the threesome had officially begun. However, before I could even react to the woman's actions Javier started stroking me really hard again. I was in a world of pain as he once again rammed his tool with powerful strokes.

"Javier, don't do it so hard!" I commanded. When he took his dick out, and tried to insert it in my ass, I really went off. "No! Stop!"

"But you said anything for me," Javier replied.

"I know, but not there, please not there," I whined like a two year old girl.

"Bitch, shut the fuck up!" another voice belted.

My anxiety level suddenly began to increase. "T-Roc, is that you?"

He removed my blindfold. "Yeah, now shut the fuck up and let me in this ass before you make my dick go soft."

"Oh my God, Javier what's going on?" I asked frantically.

Instead of answering, I couldn't believe Javier was eating me out and jerking his dick while T-Roc entered my ass. I screamed to the top of my lungs in pain as T-Roc pounded in my ass with an excruciating force. Each time he pushed his thick shaft inside, it felt like my insides were about to rip apart.

"No…please…stop!" I begged.

I couldn't believe what was happening. It was like being with Lisa in the warehouse all over again. Never in a million years did I think Javier was referring to another man, when he mentioned the word, ménage trois. T-Roc at that. Javier had certainly crossed the line.

Moments later, T-Roc's body began to shiver, which told me he was releasing himself inside of me. It was the most degrading thing I'd ever experienced in my life.

"Man ole girl got some good ass," T-Roc joked. I could tell he was pulling up his pants.

"Yo' why you do that shit man? Hell, I ain't even fucked her in her ass yet," I heard Javier say.

"Don't be mad because I got to it first," T-Roc boasted. "Thanks for the treat, Denie. You lovebirds enjoy the rest of your night."

Turning my body over, I watched as they gave each other a pound.

"I'll hit you tomorrow," T-Roc said.

As T-Roc left the room, I broke out into an uncontrollable sob.

"What's wrong, Denie?" Javier had the nerve to ask me.

"Take this shit off me now!" I screamed. After he removed the cuffs, I turned over on my back and continued to weep.

It took all the strength that I had not to try and kill the man that I'd fallen in love with. My body was in so much pain, but my heart hurt ten times more than that. When Javier came toward me, I cringed.

"Why are you all tense? Don't get your panties all in a bunch."

As I cried silently I was so mad at myself for not listening to Marisol and Rich. I ignored him as he asked me shit over and over like I had something to say.

"Man, I wish I could hear what was goin' on in that head of yours. Shit, I guess you're pissed off at me, huh? But I know you wanted it though."

"Are you serious? You know how much I hate him. I can't believe you let him do that shit to me."

"Look, you agreed to this. Don't try and make me out to be the bad guy. You know you liked him fuckin' you. Look at how freaky your ass was dancin' at the party."

"Who are you? I thought you loved me," I said in disbelief.

"Shit, I had to make you think that in order to get the revenge I needed on your precious parents. What was the likelihood of me fuckin' wit' Rich's daughter? The muthafucka who killed my sister. Shit just works out sometimes, just the way you need it too. It was fate that we saw Rich in the mall that day," he said with a huge smile.

"So, you let a man violate me just to get back at my father. You're a piece of shit, Javier!" I screamed.

"Oh, you think that was bad, wait to you see what I really have in store for you. See, there was a method to my madness. Even though you got some good pussy, I had to be careful to make sure my plan worked. After a couple of months, I think my mission has been accomplished."

I had no idea what he was talking about.

"Why Javier, how could you?"

"Easy. The passion in yo' father's eyes told me that nigga loved you, so I knew at that point I had to get back at his punkass through you…the person he probably loves the most. Finally, he'll get the payback he deserves. He has no idea what he did! Jade was all I had out here."

Fuck you and Jade. I thought to myself. He was getting so hyped, I decided not to go back and forth with him any longer. He didn't deserve a response. It was obvious that Javier didn't love me, and now I knew what I had to do.

Chapter 19

Marisol

"Who the hell is ringing my phone this early in the morning," I said irritated.

Taking off my Juicy Couture Eye Mask, I reached for my phone off the nightstand to see who had the audacity to wake me up from such a deep slumber. I didn't even bother to look at the caller ID.

"Hello."

"You have a collect call from, Lorenzo Sanchez, an inmate at…"

Not feeling like listening to the recording, I pressed 0 to accept the call. Why the hell was Renzo calling me at seven a.m. L.A. time? He knew damn well the main reason why I had Maria living with me was because I wasn't a morning person. Usually I didn't get out of bed until at least twelve unless there was something to do that usually revolved around money. I didn't even know inmates could call that early. But knowing Renzo, he probably already had several guards on his payroll. As much money as I placed in his commissary, he had enough to hire a few folks.

"Hey, Renzo," I answered half asleep.

"Good morning, Marisol. I know I probably woke you up, but I really wanted to see if you're gonna be able to come and visit me next week. I need to talk to you about some things and what's going on with my case." I could tell in his voice that he wanted answers.

"Well, it depends on if Denie is back home yet. She's still missing and I can't lose another child. I just can't."

It wasn't the real reason why I didn't want to make that trip. I'd really been avoiding him because I wasn't ready to deal with the 'I can't believe Denie is your daughter' conversation. I'd only been to visit him one time since he'd been locked up, but at the time Renzo was so hyped about his charges, he only wanted to discuss business. Even though Renzo called almost everyday, he'd yet to get the full details about how everything with Rich went down. I'd been able to avoid the discussion to some degree because the majority of the time, I always rushed him off the phone or brought up Carlos' name, which sucked up his time. By me avoiding the face to face conversations with him I was able to escape the inevitable. However, I also knew that it was only a matter of time before Renzo would ask why Rich was still alive. I needed to play my position and make sure Lorenzo knew that he could trust me until I came up with a plan.

"Well, I just…"

"Oh my God, I can't believe this, it's Denie. Hold on." I clicked over without even letting Renzo respond.

"Hello."

"Marisol, I need you. Can you please come and get me?" Denie sobbed.

"Denie, oh my gosh! Don't hang up, where are you? Why are you crying? What's wrong?" My questions wouldn't seem to stop.

"Everything is wrong."

"Denie, I can barely hear you. Where are you?"

"I'm in New York at Javier's house."

"Are you okay?"

"No."

"Give me the address so I can come and get you. Where is he? What has he done to you?"

"I gotta go, he's coming," she quickly replied.

"No, wait! Don't hang up, give me address!"

"I gotta go. I'll call you back," she whispered then hung up.

"Damn!" I said.

Realizing my daughter was in trouble, I definitely didn't have time to deal with Lorenzo, so I never clicked back over. It was obvious that she'd snuck away to call me, so I decided against calling her back. I called Rich instead. I was definitely gonna need backup.

"Yeah," he answered.

"Rich, Denie just called."

"What? Are you serious?"

"Yeah, I need you to come here ASAP. She's in New York with Javier. She's in trouble."

"In trouble? What did she say?"

"She didn't say much, but when I asked her if everything was okay she said no. She was crying and everything. I could tell that she had to sneak away just to call me. I want us to get on the road and start making our way up there until we hear back from her."

"Well, what if she doesn't call back. Marisol, you know how Denie is. What if they just had an argument or somethin'? I don't wanna go all the way up there and look like a damn fool if she makes up wit' him."

I couldn't believe how negative he was. "Rich, I'll take some of my goons from around the way if you don't think you can handle being a father for a change."

"What the hell is that supposed to mean," he said in defense mode.

"Denie would never call and ask for help if something wasn't wrong. She's just like you. Denie has too much pride for that. Look, I'll be leaving here in less than thirty minutes. You can be here by then if you want. If not, then I'll know you truly are some shit."

Not even giving him a moment to respond, I hung up on his ass. He'd pissed me off so bad I couldn't even think straight. After almost two months we'd finally heard from our daughter and Rich was acting like she'd been away at fucking summer camp. Was he really done with Denie, his pride and joy?

Jumping out of bed, I ran to the shower and took a quick bird bath before hopping back out. Grabbing the first thing I could get my hands on that was comfortable, I decided on a pair of black leggins, a black v-neck t-shirt and my hi-top Louis Vuitton sneakers. I was ready to declare war. Pulling my hair back in a ponytail, the last thing to make my outfit complete was a black baseball cap. There was no turning back now and nothing Javier could do to escape his death sentence.

Not knowing how long we would be gone, I threw some clothes into my Gucci duffel bag before grabbing Miss Pearlie. After kissing Carmen and letting Maria know that I would give her a call later, I quickly made my way toward the door. Just as I walked outside, Rich was pulling up. By getting to my house in less than twenty minutes, I guess he really did care.

Jumping in my Cayenne, Rich who was also dressed in black made his way to the passenger's side before getting in.

Wow, black tee and black no-named jeans. I know we're going to handle business, but he never wears off brand clothes, I thought. Maybe he was really fucked up.

"Did she call back?" he asked, throwing his bag in the back seat.

"No," I said being short.

At this point I didn't really want to talk to him. I was still pissed at how negative his ass was earlier.

We barely said two words to each other as we rode in silence all the way through the Baltimore Tunnel. That is until my choice of music finally began to annoy him.

"Why the hell are we listenin' to Nicki Minaj? How old

are you again?" he asked sarcastically.

Not feeding into him, I ignored his comment then turned the radio up even louder. He stared at me for a few seconds before laying his seat back like he was trying to take a nap. But by the time we passed the Chesapeake House rest area, he couldn't take it any longer.

"Can you please put on somethin' else? What about some grown folks music like Maze or Raheem, shit I don't even care if it's Luther. I'm just tired of hearin' this shit."

"I don't give a fuck what you're tired of hearing. This is my vehicle and you can get…"

My phone rang right while I was about to dig into Rich's shit. Although the call was from a blocked number, I answered the phone anyway.

"Hello."

"Marisol, it's me. He left to go to the store."

"Denie. I'm so glad you called back. Where are you?"

"I don't know Javier's address. I just know how to get here."

"Let me speak to her," Rich interrupted.

"No, I got this," I said, cutting my eye at him for opening his mouth. I didn't want Denie to be upset that I was bringing him and hang up the phone.

"Where are you Marisol? Is that Rich?"

"Yes. Umm we'll be at the Delaware Memorial Bridge shortly. I left as soon as I could."

"Why did you bring him?" she questioned.

"Denie, I needed back up. I didn't know what to expect when I got there. The most important thing is that we both love you and we're coming to get you regardless."

"I ain't nobody's back up," Rich interrupted again.

"Rich please!" I yelled. "Denie, do you wanna tell me what happened?"

"I just wanna come home. I feel humiliated." When she started to cry, I knew it must've been serious.

"Sweetheart, what happened?"

Denie wouldn't respond.

"Denie, where are you? Go look on a piece of mail. You should be able to get the address from there." After all this time I'd known Javier, I certainly didn't know where he lived. That nigga changed houses like he changed his underwear.

"Okay, hold on."

"No, stay on the phone with me and go look," I demanded.

A few minutes later, Denie blurted out the address. As Rich entered the location into the navigation, I listened to my daughter cry as if she'd lost all hope.

"Maybe I should just leave while he's gone," she said.

"No, you have to just stay there. That's the best way we'll be able to find him. Plus we need him to be comfortable. Don't worry, we'll be there soon," I said, pushing the speaker button to calm Rich's antsy-ass down.

"But what if he makes me do it again?"

"Do what? Denie what happened, tell me?" Rich questioned.

"He made me...I mean"

"What did he do?" Rich blurted out.

Denie continued to ball. "It was awful. I had to act as if I liked it, but then...take me off speaker."

"Okay you're off. What else did he do?" I asked as Rich leaned over the console and tried to eavesdrop.

"Him and his friend, they made me..."

"What Denie?"

After trying to get the story out of her before Javier returned, it was obvious that she was too broken up about it to go into details at the moment.

"Okay so the navigation is saying that we'll be there in two hours and seventeen minutes. Now listen Denie...make sure the door is unlocked. It's important that no matter what you do, that door stays unlocked so we can get in. Do you understand?"

"Yes. Please hurry, Ma," Denie said right before the phone went dead.

My mind suddenly began to race as I pressed my foot down and started going well over ninety miles per hour. I needed to get to my baby. There was no way I was ever gonna let another one of my children down. I didn't know the extent of what happened, but I knew my child's life was at risk. I wasn't about to lose another loved one.

"Marisol, slow down. I just saw a State Trooper," Rich advised. "We can't help her if we don't get there in one piece."

Slowly letting my foot off the gas, I finally broke down.

"Rich, she called me, Ma. Oh my God. She's never called me that."

Realizing that I was no longer in any position to drive, Rich had me pull over so we could switch positions. I was a mess. I had to get to Denie. There was no way I was gonna allow her to be apart of Javier's sick vendetta against me and Rich. My baby had already experienced so much pain in her life. She didn't deserve this.

✶✶✶✶✶✶✶✶✶✶✶✶✶✶

We rode in complete silence until the navigation said, "*you have arrived at your destination.*"

At that point, both of us knew it was time to put in work, and there was no doubt everyone was leaving unharmed except Javier. Rich and I worked out the details of how we would handle things once we scoped out his spot. We noticed there was a back alley with fire escapes and wondered if we should try entering the house that way, but decided against it since we didn't want to draw any unwanted attention. My goal was to kill this nigga real quick, get my daughter, and be out.

After driving around the block a few times, we finally decided to park in the alley and walk around to the front. Attaching the silencers to our guns before getting out the car, Rich and I looked like a modern day Bonnie and Clyde.

As soon as I saw this lady coming out of the building, I quickly ran up to catch the door. Rich came behind me a few seconds later. We started engaging in fake, heavy conversation while walking past the security guard even though his fat-ass was reading a newspaper and not paying us any attention anyway. We ended up taking the stairs instead of the elevator to get a better feel for the building. Twelve flights later, we were on the penthouse level. Rich was out of breath since he was a tad bit out of shape, but I was fine. The treadmill was a way of life for me so climbing stairs was nothing, especially since I was hyped and ready to put a cap in Javier's ass.

After Rich got it together we peeked down the hall to make sure the coast was clear before placing our ears against the door. Almost immediately, we could hear Denie crying.

"No Javier, please stop!" she screamed.

"Tell me who the fuck you called or I'ma let him do it again!" Javier shouted.

Rich and I were both hot headed, but we knew if either one of us lost control, it could cost our daughter's life, so we had to remain calm as Javier continued to yell. Giving each other one final look, Rich slowly opened the door.

I can't wait to put your fucking blood all over this white carpet, I thought to myself, as we quietly made our way inside.

From the direction of their voices we could tell they were upstairs, so both Rich and I took our time climbing each step. Luckily, the T.V. was on so just in case we made a slight noise it would've been drowned out.

When we finally reached the top step and made our way to the bedroom, I couldn't believe what I was watching. Javier had my baby girl tied to the bed, while some thugged out looking nigga had his way with her. No longer able to control his anger, Rich immediately zapped out and starting beating the shit out of dude with his gun.

"Ahh shit!" The naked dude yelled as Rich pistol whipped him.

In that one moment I was weak and Javier caught me slipping. I froze, which was a bad move because Javier was able to tackle me causing my gun to fly across the floor.

"Muthafucka, get off her!" Rich yelled as he came to my rescue.

Suddenly, I noticed the guy trying to escape out the window. Standing up, I tried my best to get to him, but his ass jumped out onto the fire escape so fast, I never got a chance. It was like he'd done that shit before. By the time I made it to the window, I watched as he quickly made his way down, then haul ass down the street...naked and all.

"Damn!" I was pissed that I'd let him get away.

"Ma, help me," Denie cried.

"Ahhhh!" Rich yelled when Javier bit him on his arm. "Shoot his ass, Marisol. Shoot him!" he belted as they continued to scuffle

I ran over to get my gun off of the floor before pointing it in Javier's direction. Hitting him in the arm at first, I let off around round which landed in his chest. It was definitely enough to slow him down.

I stood over Javier as his naked body squirmed on the floor.

"Javier why?" I asked, pointing Miss Pearlie at him.

"Marisol, where's your loyalty. You let this nigga kill Jade and you ain't do shit about it." Javier looked at Rich's gun on the floor. "See a .45. My sister was killed wit' a .45. You dumb enough to keep the murder weapon, nigga!" he shouted at Rich.

"Fuck you. I didn't even know your sister was dead. I don't know who killed her, but I do know who killed you," I said, pointing the gun to his head as Rich worked on untying Denie.

"Wait let me say somethin' don't shoot. Denie told me what he did. She told me everything. That muthafucka killed Carlos, too!"

"You're a liar!" I yelled then looked back at my daughter. "Denie, is he telling the truth?"

She paused for what seemed like forever, then finally spoke. "Kill him, he's lying," Denie said as Rich stared at her in disbelief.

I wasn't sure what that look was for. Was it because of what Javier said or was it the fact that for once they were both on the same side.

"So, Denie you wanna play like that? After all I did for you…all the shit I gave you. That's okay, you'll gets yours, too. You'll see," Javier said as he began to cough up blood.

"Handle that nigga or I will!" Rich yelled.

"It don't matter if I die today. Denie will never be able to forget me. Remember everybody gotta die even…"

Before Javier could finish his sentence I gave him two bullets in the head. He was done torturing my daughter once and for all.

Chapter 20

Rich

"Can you watch Juanita for me while I go and handle this Lisa shit?" I asked Marisol as she walked out of her master bathroom.

Even though Juanita was dyin' to play wit' Carmen, I wanted Marisol to see her sweet innocent face, so she couldn't say no.

"Are you crazy? Where's her mother?"

"She's at the salon and you know I don't like Juanita bein' up there all day, listenin' to them bitches gossip."

"That's not my problem," Marisol responded.

I knew she didn't have anything against Juanita. It was Trixie that she had a problem wit'.

"Come on, Marisol. I can't take her wit' me." I poked out my lips. "Please."

I knew if I brought up the fact that Maria was really gonna be the one watchin' her, Marisol would've went off on me.

She rolled her eyes into the back of her head. "Alright,

but I have shit to do today so don't be long."

"Cool, I'll be back before umm...around six."

"Rich, don't fucking lie. I got some important shit to do, so please be here on time."

Before I could respond Denie came out of the bathroom in her towel.

"Hi Denie," Juanita said, happy to see her sister that always treated her like shit.

"What is she doing here?" Denie asked. She gave Juanita a disgusted look. She didn't even speak.

I'd never seen a nineteen year old jealous of a three year old.

"Denie, don't treat your sister like that," I said in disbelief.

"You mean your daughter," Denie shot back.

"Well, maybe you wouldn't feel that way if you hung out with us sometime and got to know her," I responded.

"I don't have to get to know anybody," Denie said as she left the room mumblin' shit under her breath.

"I'll be glad when you stop actin' like a bitch!" I shouted.

Marisol frowned. "Rich, was that really necessary?"

"What? I'm serious. Denie's attitude is gettin' on my fuckin' nerves."

"So what. It's no need to call her that. She hasn't been herself since we got back from New York, so I've just been trying to give her space."

"Well, good for you. She's not actin' like a bitch toward you, so maybe you don't understand."

"So, Trixie allows you to talk like that in front of her?" Marisol pointed to Juanita.

"Look, I don't need any partenin' advice. Besides, you left your daughter, remember?"

I could see steam comin' out of Marisol's ears. "Fuck you. Can you please stop bringing that shit up?"

I smiled. "Oh, so it's okay for you to curse, but I can't?"

As Marisol rolled her eyes again, I thought back to

Denie's disrespectful ways again. No matter how angry she was at me, I couldn't believe she'd sold me out by tellin' Javier about me killin' Los. However, on the flip side, the most important thing was when she told Marisol Javier was lying about the whole thing. I wondered if she'd done that for me or to get back at Javier. Although I didn't understand why she decided to have my back all of a sudden, I was appreciative for her loyalty.

"Let me go. Again, I'll be back by six."

"Not a minute later, Rich," Marisol replied. "Oh, by the way, just give Denie time. I'm sure she'll eventually come around. You just gotta have patience."

"I guess."

When Marisol let her hard exterior down it was so sexy to me. I gave her a kiss on her forehead and then on her lips.

"Aww. I'ma tell Mommy," Juanita snickered. She'd never seen me kiss anyone outside of Trixie.

"Juanita, go ahead downstairs wit' Carmen and play."

"Okay Daddy," she said, grabbin' her Juicy Couture backpack that contained her Vtech MobiGo System and Dora the Explorer doll.

"You can leave the bag here, just take your stuff," I said.

After grabbin' the two toys, Juanita finally left.

I turned to Marisol. "So, you miss me?" I asked tryin' to kiss her again.

"So, you still fucking Trixie?"

I shook my head. "Hell no. You know I just consider her my baby's mother. Why you trippin'?"

"I'm not tripping. I'm just asking a simple question." Marisol stared me down before continuin'. "Your time is ticking away. Go handle your business, so you can come back and pick up your child."

Lookin' at Marisol's sexy frame, my dick started to get hard. "Damn, it's been a minute. I miss you."

"Whatever! Bye Rich."

Not wantin' to push her too much before she changed her mind, I decided to leave enough well alone and roll out. As I jumped in my car and headed toward my house, it felt good not to be goin' to my mother's spot. Hittin' the button for my radio, as soon as I turned to 96.3, I couldn't believe Luther Vandross' song, *A House is Not a Home* was on. The shit was too coincidental.

"When I climb the stairs and turn the key ohh please be there," Luther sung wit' his smooth balladeer voice.

That was my song, even though I didn't need a bitch to make my house a home. It felt good to have my shit back, even if I was going to be there alone. As I pulled into my driveway several minutes later, all of a sudden a police car pulled up behind me.

What the fuck is this about, I thought lookin' through my rearview.

I wasn't in the mood for any bullshit. Gettin' out of my car, I waited as the short, white cop got out of his. He walked up on me wit' so much attitude, it was kind of hilarious. You could tell he had a little man's complex. I was givin' him 5'6', but he might've been shorter.

"Juan Sanchez?"

"Yes, little man," I couldn't help myself.

"Excuse me," he responded wit' a huge frown.

"Oh, my bad. Yes, Officer."

He handed me an envelope. "You've been served," he said, then walked back to his cruiser.

"Served...for what?" I asked as he pulled off.

Thinkin' it was best for me to open the envelope once I got inside, I quickly opened the door and disabled the alarm, then immediately sat down the livin' room. I couldn't wait to see what this shit was about.

My eyes immediately enlarged as I scanned the document. "Probate court, what the fuck?"

My dumb-ass mother-in-law was obviously tryin' to take me to court to fight for the house. That bitch had really bumped her head if she thought she was gettin' the piece of property that I'd worked so hard for. I couldn't dial her number fast enough.

"I take it you got your paperwork," was the first thing First Lady said. "I've been expecting your call."

"Any other time I would'a been ready to pay you a visit for involvin' my name in this shit, but I'ma choose the high road this time."

She chuckled. "That's a first."

"Well, bitch the joke is actually on you. If you would've done your research you would know that your coke sniffin' daughter was too busy usin' drugs that she never placed the deed solely in her name once our divorce was finalized. The house was still in my mother's name, and since I inherited my mother's estate, the house is good as mine."

"I don't believe you," she responded.

"I don't give a damn what you believe. If you still wanna waste your money by goin' to court, then go ahead. It's gonna be fun watchin' your ass lose."

"Rich, you can't do this! Lisa would be devastated to know that you were tryin' to take everything back. And when the hell are you gonna send me my stuff? I still haven't gotten anything yet!"

"I'll send that bullshit when I get ready," I said, then hung up the phone. It felt good to get back at her wicked-ass after the way she'd treated me all these years.

Already in a good mood, I decided to call the insurance company to get an update on the status of my check. My money issues were so close to bein' over I could taste it. Wit' that amount of legit money, I was gonna be able to live even better than before. My first stop was gonna be the Bentley dealership.

"I gotta get me a black Bentley Coupe," I announced then looked around the house. "I'ma throw all this shit away and get the whole house remodeled, too. I don't want nothin' re-mindin' me of Lisa."

Grabbin' my phone from off the table, I dialed the 1-800 number that I'd already stored in my contacts list. After listenin' to one of those annoyin' ass automated machines tellin' me to push this and that, someone finally came on the line.

"Thanks for calling Global Life. How may I help you?" the woman greeted in a soft tone.

"Hello, this is Mr. Juan Sanchez. I'm callin' in regards to my insurance policy pay out."

"Do you have your account number, Mr. Sanchez?"

"Yes, it's 40710084271105."

She typed in the information. "Okay. This policy was under Lisa Sanchez, correct?"

"Yes ma'am, that's correct. She was my wife. She passed away a few weeks ago. I'm Juan Sanchez, her beneficiary."

"I'm sorry to hear that, sir." I could hear her typin' more shit into the computer. "Can you provide me with Mrs. Sanchez's social security number and address? We need that verify the account."

"I sure can," I said, givin' her the information. "So, how's your day goin'?"

"Going good so far. How about yours?" she asked still typing.

"Mine is goin' great." The shit was about to be goin' even better once she told me when my check was bein' mailed out.

"Okay, Mr. Sanchez, I've pulled up the account."

"So, I am the beneficiary on her policy correct?"

"Correct."

A smile quickly flashed across my face. "So, I'm sure by now you all have gotten her death certificate, autopsy report or whatever else you need, so do you have any idea when my benefit payment will be mailed."

"Well, Mr. Sanchez I'm afraid I have some bad news," she stated.

The smile instantly disappeared. "Bad news? What are you talkin' about, lady?"

"Mrs. Sanchez hadn't paid the premium on this policy in almost a year, nine months to be exact, so the account is inactive."

My heart rate began to increase. "Inactive. What the fuck

do you mean inactive?"

"Sir, the policy was cancelled due to failure of payment. I see here that we have sent several cancellation notices to the address on file and have not received..."

I was so fuckin' blown as I hung up in that bitches face. I picked up the first thing I could get my hands on, which was Lisa's Waterford crystal elephant that was on the table. Pieces flew everywhere as I threw the three hundred dollar piece of shit she collected against the wall. Just when I thought everything was goin' to get better for me, somethin' always went wrong. I could see that bitch Lisa now lookin' down on me laughin' her ass off. I couldn't believe she'd stopped makin' the payments.

Mad as hell, I left out the house, jumped in my car and just started drivin'. Desperately needin' some air or a fuckin' drink, I found myself on the highway drivin' wit' no destination when my phone rang.

"Yeah," I answered extremely irritated.

"Hey, Rich."

"Who the hell is this?"

"It's Honey. I guess since we haven't talked in so long you don't even know my voice anymore."

"Oh, shit what's up, Honey?" I tried my best to act excited, but she couldn't have called at a worse time.

"I was just thinkin' about you. I would love to see you."

"Really, well let me just tell you now, if you lookin' for money, then you might as well call another nigga because I'm fucked up right now."

"Have I said anything about money? I just really wanna see you. I miss you," she replied in a sweet manner.

"Well, if that's the case, what are you doin' now?"

That's all I needed. If she was willin' to sell me some free pussy, then I was definitely buyin'.

I was already on I-95, so it didn't take me any time to get to Baltimore and head toward the Harbor. Honey already had a hotel room at Pier 5. I knew her freak-ass had probably fucked already and had the room left over from another trick, but I didn't even care. Wit' all the tension I had built up, I needed some ass.

Once I pulled up to valet, I checked my phone under her text messages to see what the room number was again and made my way up to the 3rd floor. Once I knocked on the door, Honey answered within seconds. She looked fine as shit. Her caramel brown complexion was still flawless and no longer did she look like a whore, she looked like money. She'd definitely upgraded her lingerie game and was in Gucci now instead of that cheap Frederick's of Hollywood shit she used to wear. Her weave was long as hell and the bang gave her a new look. Everyone had always mistaken her for Meagan Good, and now she really looked like her.

"So, what's been up, Rich," she said, walking away from me in her six-inch heels, toward the bed.

"Life has thrown me a lot of curve balls lately. You called me at the right time because I really needed this."

"Needed what? This good pussy." Honey sat on the edge of the bed, exposin' her cleanly shaved nest.

"Damn, you got some new piercings, huh?"

"Yes, and it makes me climax to no end."

"You look different."

"Well, there are a lot of things different about me, Rich. I had some work done. I got some new implants, but this is still my natural ass. I been doin' squats. It's soft see, feel it."

Her breasts did look bigger and her ass was nice and plump. I got closer and palmed her backside.

"You seem different, too," I said.

"The pussy just got better, that's all. Feel it. I'm wet as shit," she said, placin' my hand inside of her.

As I inserted one finger, then two, she let out a soft moan.

"Rich, I missed you. Don't stay away from me like that anymore. You could fuck me for free anytime you want. I'll never forget all you did for me when times were hard."

Were hard? Huh, the bitch must've come up on some money, I thought to myself. I wondered how much.

The more she spoke, the more I moved my finger back and forth. By now, her nest was drenched.

"She's ready," I said, removin' my hand.

As hard as my dick was, that let me know I was ready, too. As I took off my jeans and removed my phone from the holster, Honey already had already pushed my boxers down and placed my shit in her mouth.

"Damn, baby. Hold up," I said, throwin' the phone on the bed. I needed it near me just in case Marisol called about Juanita.

As Honey began her deep throat routine, my dick found its way back to that warm pocket that I missed. Her head game was on point.

"That's right baby suck it," I said, thrustin' my dick toward the back of her throat.

Honey came up for air. "You like it."

"I love it."

As Honey placed my shaft inside her mouth, I reached down and grabbed her head. Moments later, the tinglin' started in my toes, then made it's way up my leg at a rapid pace. I could feel the cum at the tip of dick, right before I released all in her mouth.

From the bed to the floor, we ended up fuckin' all over the hotel room before collapsin' into each other's arms a few hours later. Honey no longer was the whore that I used to trick off from the strip club. She was a potential contender for my roster. Honey obviously had her shit together and was about her paper and for her to say that she didn't need me to pay her anymore, she'd had a come up from somewhere. For all the money she'd tricked off me over the years, she might've had enough money to go around now. Since I'd ran out the house without my gun, I couldn't jack her this time, but I'd be back to collect.

It was gettin' late. I knew I'd told Marisol I would be

there to get Juanita by six, but since she wasn't givin' up no pussy, and I couldn't pass up the good shit right in front of me, Juanita would have to stay a little longer. My phone continued to ring over the next few minutes. I'm sure it was Marisol blowin' me up and cursin' me out at the same time. When I looked up at the clock on the nightstand, and it read 9:03 p.m., I knew my name was mud. Shit, I was already three hours late, but Honey was worth Marisol beefin' wit' me for a couple of days.

Chapter 21

Marisol

"Ohh shit I'm about to cum, Rich I'm about to cum."
"Me too, baby."
"I can't believe this!" I yelled, playing that shit back over in my mind.

Rich had bumped his motherfucking head. When my phone rung and I saw his number I thought he was calling to ask me to keep Juanita longer followed by some type of excuse. Little did he or I know that his phone had obviously called me by mistake. I knew it. He was still fucking Trixie and I felt stupid once again for falling into his trap. Those bastards had me fucked up though if they thought my nanny was gonna babysit while they had a damn fuck fest. They were probably laying up in bed laughing at me the whole time I was calling.

"Maria! Maria!" I yelled.

"Yes, Miss Marisol," she hurried in my room as I slipped on some shorts and a t-shirt.

I didn't bother with my hair since I was in such a hurry, but one thing I didn't forget was Miss Pearlie. I threw her in my

Chanel Leo bag, ready to fuck something up. Looking in Juanita's bag, I was able to get Trixie's address off of some day-care form that she went to.

"I need to leave out for a while."

"Is everything okay."

"It will be. Where's Juanita?"

"She's in the kitchen drinking a Capri Sun with Carmen," Maria informed.

"Good."

After picking up her bag, I ran downstairs to the kitchen and grabbed Juanita by the collar of her shirt.

"What did she do?" Carmen asked with a surprised look.

"We not fighting, Miss Marisol," Juanita added.

She looked scared as I ushered her toward the door without saying a word, but I didn't care. She could blame her parents for interrupting her little play date.

Once we got in the car, I looked in the backseat. "Put your seat belt on, lil' girl," I ordered. "And stop crying. It's not your fault that your father is an asshole!"

As I tore out of my driveway, I looked at my Chanel J12 watch. It was 9:45 p.m. and that bastard had yet to call. Trixie and Rich were definitely gonna get the surprise of their lives when I interrupted their sex session.

I made it to Ft. Washington in no time, becoming angrier by the second the closer I got to her house. I pulled in the driveway a few minutes later, Rich's car was no where in sight.

He's probably parked in the garage, I told myself.

"You can take your seat belt off now," I told Juanita who hadn't said a word since we left.

After putting the gun in my pocket and helping her out the car, we walked up the front door, with me ringing the doorbell at least ten times. When that didn't work, I started knocking like the fucking police.

When Trixie finally opened the door looking like she was half sleep, I raised my hand and slapped the shit out of her.

"Aighhh. What the fuck is your problem, Marisol?"

Trixie asked as she shielded herself from my next two blows.

Juanita continued to cry. "Mommy."

"Bitch, where the fuck is Rich?" I asked. I had plans on pulling Miss Pearlie out if she wanted to play dumb.

Trixie held out her arm. "Juanita, come in the house, baby. Go to your room."

As the little girl took off running, Trixie made sure her daughter was out of harms way before she turned back to me. "Did you hurt my daughter?"

"No, I didn't! Now, where's Rich?" I repeated.

"I don't know! Damn, what the fuck is going on?"

Furious, I pulled the .380 out and pointed it toward her face. "Bitch, stop playing stupid. Y'all got me watching your daughter while y'all over here fucking! Where is he?"

"Marisol please, I swear, he's not here! I just got home from work. What the hell is wrong with you?" She looked scared as hell.

"His phone accidently called me and I heard him fucking somebody! Are you covering up for him?"

Trixie quickly shook her head. "No. You can call anybody at my salon and ask them. I just left not to long ago."

Normally, Trixie was a shit talker, but I guess anybody would change their tune with a gun pointed in their direction.

"Ugghhhh!" I yelled mad as shit. I couldn't believe I'd let her see me like this over that no good nigga.

As bad as I wanted to apologize my pride wouldn't allow me to. I finally lowered the gun.

"So, when was the last time you talked to him?"

"I haven't heard from Rich since he left this morning. He said he was taking Juanita to the zoo," Trixie responded.

"Well, your daughter has been at my house all day."

"That lying muthafucka."

"So, are you and Rich still fucking?" I asked.

"We're not just fucking, we're together. He sleeps here with me almost every night."

I bit the inside of my mouth to try and calm myself

down. "I just asked him were you all sleeping together and he said you were just his baby's mother. Wow."

"Oh yeah! If that's the case then why is some of his stuff in the drawers up stairs? He's lying to you," Trixie added. "So, wait a minute, y'all still fool with each other?"

"When I feel like it. He just tried to get some earlier, but I turned him down."

Now more than ever I hated Rich for making me look like a dumb-ass fool. He was gonna pay for humiliating me in front of trash like Trixie. Then it dawned on me. While she was mad at him, this was the perfect opportunity to get the information I needed about Carlos. My pride had to be put to the side for now as I fished for information.

"Look Trixie, I'm sorry for attacking you like that in front of your daughter, but I've been through a lot lately. I don't know if Rich had told you all we've been through this past year."

"All I know is that the Sanchez's have been dropping like flies and I told Rich I didn't want my daughter around all that shit."

"Did he ever tell you what happened to Carlos?"

"No, he didn't. He never wants to talk about it," Trixie said.

"Well, all I know is that when I catch that nigga it's on and popping. I ain't nobody's joke."

"If he wasn't fucking me or you tonight, then I wonder who you heard him with?"

"I'm about to find out."

I was pissed off as I stormed away from Trixie's house and got in the car on a war path. Rich was foolish if his ass thought he was gonna keep betraying me and get away with it.

He's probably at his mother's house with that bitch, I thought to myself as I peeled out of Trixie's development and made my way back in the city.

Rage consumed my body as I pictured him fucking me and Trixie at the same time. *Was I the new Lisa?* Thinking about how he'd destroyed her life, I became even more furious for allowing Rich to play me for a fool.

Hopping on the Beltway, I took my Porsche to the limit as I headed toward I-295 at top speed. Hoping there were no police around, I banged on the steering wheel and cursed Rich out all the way to his mother's house. There was no way he was getting away with this. Once I pulled up to the house, I looked for the spare key he'd given me in my purse, which I quickly located on my Tiffany keychain. He wanted to make sure that I always had copy for emergency purposes, and as far as I was concerned, this was one hell of an emergency.

I got out the truck and ran around to the back of the house to see if there were any vehicles trying to be incognito. Although his mother's old beat up Toyota was back there, and his Range wasn't, I was still convinced that he was inside.

That broke muthafucka can't afford to pay the maintenance fees on that Range anyway, so the shit might be on the side of the road. Hell, it's a possibility that he might be driving his mother's car.

Making my way back to the front of the house, I took out my gun just in case I needed to put a cap in his ass. I was gonna show Rich that I meant business. Not even being discrete or trying to be quiet, I put the key in and unlocked the door.

"Rich! You bitch-ass nigga I know you in here! I'm gonna show you not to fuck with me!" I yelled through the house.

I looked through every room on the main level, but he wasn't there. After running up the stairs, I checked both of the guest rooms along with the bathroom in the hallway first, but he still couldn't be found.

"Where the hell are you?"

Walking into his room, the first thing I did was check the bathroom. After realizing he wasn't in there either, I made my way toward the bed that was neatly made, and didn't look disturbed. At that point I was convinced that he hadn't come to his mother's house to fuck, however, there were some women's clothing scattered all over the floor like she'd been in a hurry.

"Maybe they were here, but left," I said.

Picking up one of the shirts, I was surprised when I realized that it belonged to me. When I noticed my Alexander Wang racerback tank, along with my Hudson skinny jeans that's when I knew all that shit was mine. Scanning the room, my eyes grew the size of Texas when I noticed a Louis Vuitton suitcase sitting in front of his closet. My heart beat was so loud, it sounded like that shit was about to jump out of my chest.

As I walked over and flipped the top of the suitcase back, my initials MGS, immediately stared back at me. It was the suitcase I had the morning of the robbery.

*God no. It can't b*e, I thought to myself.

I was furious and hurt at the same time. Chills covered my body as I shook my head in disbelief. Where was the loyal man that I loved? Digging for more evidence, I decided to look in his closet to see if there was anything else to prove he was there, and once I saw the blood stained New Balance I was convinced that Rich had robbed me.

My heart felt heavy as thoughts about that morning ran through my mind. This man was foul and now more than ever I felt like Rich had to die.

Chapter 22

When I woke up this morning, I was tired of looking like shit. Feeling extremely depressed, I didn't have much of an appetite since we'd gotten back from New York, so I knew I'd lost a few pounds. My emotions were mixed. I hated Javier for what he'd done to me, but I missed what we had before everything went downhill.

Maybe my mother and Chanel were right. I needed to go out and enjoy myself. Chanel had been calling me like crazy, but I'd been ducking her calls. I finally broke down and answered earlier today, and agreed to go out to Pure Lounge with her later on to make up for lost times. Since I'd lost myself and I looked like a train wreck, I called to see if Jermaine could bring me back to life. From the urgency in my voice, I'm sure Jermaine knew it was an emergency, so he agreed to do my hair, which was exactly what I needed to boost my spirits.

As I finally peeled myself out of bed, I looked in the mirror and was disgusted at the image staring back. Now, I could see what my mother was talking about. Dark circles had taken over my eyes and the bags underneath them made matters even worse. There was no way in hell anybody was gonna mistake me for Lauren London right about now. I was gonna get back, and I'm sure Jermaine was gonna help make that happen.

After getting out of the shower, I mixed baby oil and lavender lotion together and put it all over my body. I couldn't remember the last time lotion felt so good, which meant I was in need of some true pampering. After putting my panties on, all I could do was shake my head. This damn depression wasn't doing too good on my body because my ass was starting to get smaller. Thank God I still had my breasts though, but my ass was what I loved most. Not that I was trying to get with anybody anytime soon, but I just wanted to love myself again when I looked in the mirror.

Knowing the July air was really hot outside, I slipped on my Shadyboots t-shirt, Rock & Republic jeans, and Tory Burch flip flops. After grabbing my Louis Vuitton bum bag I strapped it around my waist then threw in all my girlie essentials, and my cell phone. I headed out the door moments later.

It felt like I was in Miami when I left out of the house because that summer rain was playing peek-a-boo not knowing if it wanted to pour down or let the sun shine. I decided to drive my mother's 650 BMW convertible since she never drove it anyway and if the sun would stay out long enough, I could stunt around the city. Once I pulled out of the gate and was out of our bougie neighborhood, I put my Kanye West CD on blast. The *Monster* remix with Nicki Minaj and Jay-Z was my jam. As soon as I got in my Nicki mode my phone started ringing, which pissed me off. It was a blocked number again. I'd been getting calls from an unknown number for about a week now and it was getting on my nerves because they never said anything. They just listened to my voice and hung up. Irritated as ever, I answered the phone.

"Yeah"

"Bitch, you have no idea what you've done. I'm gonna get your ass…"*Click*

Before I could even respond to curse her ass out, she hung up on me. It was probably somebody's baby mother or girlfriend that I'd fucked in the past.

When my phone rang a few seconds later, this time I was gonna be ready.

"Bitch, take your beef up with your dude!" I yelled into the phone.

"You have a collect call from... Nelson White, an inmate at a correctional facility. To refuse this call, hang up. If you accept this call dial 0," the automated operator stated.

I let out a huge sigh before hitting zero. I wasn't in the mood for Nelson's shit right now.

"Thank you. This call is subject to recording," the operator continued.

"Damn, you finally decided to accept my call!" Nelson barked.

"Look, calm down," I said irritated that I even picked up the phone.

"What the fuck do you mean calm down? You ain't been answerin' my calls for a minute. So, you gettin' brand new now since you fuckin' wit' that New York dude. Yeah, I heard about that shit."

"I don't fuck with nobody."

"Yeah, I bet you don't after somebody killed his faggot-ass. When he was locked up, they say he was fuckin' with those boys. Since when you start likin' gay mufuckas?"

"Whatever. What did you call me for, because I don't have time for this shit?"

"What the fuck is up wit' you, Denie? Man, you used to love me. What happened to us?"

"You went to jail and left me out here by myself that's what happened. If you hadn't rolled out, life wouldn't be so fucked up."

"That was all Rich's doing. You changed Denie. Your obsession to make your mother pay consumed you. You were so angry and bitter."

I was furious. "I can't believe you just said that. Didn't you see all that shit I went through? Damn, one minute you say I'm strong. The next minute you're saying I'm bitter. You know what Nelson…go fuck yourself. And lose my damn number!"

Hanging up on his ass, I let out a loud scream and turned my music up. Nelson wasn't gonna fuck up my day with that hating shit. I made it to the salon in less than twenty minutes. As I stood outside and rang the bell to be buzzed in, of course it started raining again. Finally Pam, the owner of the shop let me in.

"Hey Denie, how you been?" she asked with a huge smile.

"Good, and you?"

"Girl, I've been good, dealing with my daughter's senior prom stuff. Those shades are hot," she said, eying my Chrome Heart sunglasses.

"Thanks. Is Jermaine upstairs?"

"Yeah, he's up there, but I need you to sign in. I'll call upstairs to see if he wants Travena to get you started down here."

"Okay, thank you," I replied.

"No problem."

I had a seat in the waiting area until Travena, Jermaine's assistant, was ready to start on my hair. Usually the salon was packed, but you know how Black people are. When the rain starts coming down, they think twice about getting their hair done. A little rain wasn't about to stop me though.

After Travena washed my hair and put me under the dryer, I was soon ready to be styled and curled. When I walked in Jermaine's suite he looked fabulous as usual in his white v-neck tee, some distressed jeans, and a Gucci belt that matched his red and blue Gucci sandals.

"Hey, Girl, where you been?" he questioned.

"I was in New York for a while."

"Okay, I need to hear all about it. Oh, before we get into all that, how you want your hair?"

"I want a Nicki Minaj bang."

"Girl no. All the cunts are rocking that look. How bout I give you the Janet Jackson Pleasure Principle bang."

I giggled. "Whatever you think."

"Now, getting back to you being MIA. You didn't even invite me. Damn, you know how much I love New York." He drew an oversized heart in the air being dramatic. "Why didn't you tell me you was up there, we could've hung out together?"

"Well…umm.."

"Oh, I get it. You were up there with the trade, huh? Girl, who you was messing with up top?"

"This dude named Javier, but we're over now though."

"Javier…Javier. That name sounds so familiar. Is he Puerto Rican?"

I nodded my head. "Yeah, why, cuz' you think you know everybody?"

"Hold up, yeah…Javier. You talking about Camielle's baby father? Please don't tell me that's the same Javier."

I shrugged my shoulders. "His baby mother died, but I don't remember her name."

"That's him. Girl, you know how she died right, her and the son," he said, twirling me around as he trimmed my hair.

"He told me that they died in a car accident."

"No, girl. Word is they died of HIV complications. The baby died when he was born and then the wife died soon after of pneumonia." Jermaine was just about to trim another piece when he stopped. "Denie, please tell me that you used a condom."

"Jermaine, please stop it. I can't handle this shit." Getting an instant heartache, I still couldn't wrap my head around the HIV comment.

"Look, this is serious. I usually don't get in people's business, but you're like family and I would never keep anything like that from you."

I was in a state of shock, but tried to maintain my composure. Maybe it was shop talk and all rumors. "Maybe we're talking about two different Javier's."

"I doubt it. If he looks like…what's that guy name on The Game. Umm…Malik. The football player who was on drugs. The Javier I'm talking about looks just like him. Word on the street is that this thug dude was sweet on Javier. Bought him a car and everything."

"Are you serious?" I asked swallowing the lump in my throat.

"Girl yeah, a couple of queens I know who live in New York told me about him. Apparently, the thug dude got Javier back on his feet because he used to run with the queens doing all the credit cards and check schemes. They said that thug queen laid Javier's place out. I heard it was all white or something."

Instantly, it felt like I was going to throw up. As Jermaine went on and on as he did my hair, all I could think of was how close Javier's mouth was to T-Roc's balls when we had that disgusting threesome. Javier…gay? The shit seemed unbelievable. Then I thought about what Nelson said. Maybe he wasn't hating and was really telling the truth. Did Javier have HIV, too? At that moment, so many things came back to me. I should've known. That flu that he had the entire time we were together, and that dry cough he just couldn't get rid of. Not to mention, that weight loss. All that time, I thought his ass was just metro sexual. Closing my eyes, I said a prayer hoping this was all just a bad dream. Maybe it was just rumors.

Looking in the full length mirror, something came over me and I just couldn't take it any longer.

"Jermaine, I gotta go."

"Girl, you not leaving out of here with your head half way done. I got a rep to uphold. Demi Mode clients walk out of this door fierce. They turn heads all up and down Georgia Avenue."

"I feel sick Jermaine, I gotta…"

All of a sudden I started throwing up everywhere. I didn't even make it to the bathroom. Grabbing my bag, I stumbled down the stairs as I listened to Jermaine cuss and fuss about who was gonna clean the mess up. I didn't care about my hair or his reputation at the moment, all I cared about was the awful things that Jermaine had just told me about Javier.

Please God, make Jermaine's sources be unreliable, for once…

Once I left out of the shop, I walked a couple of feet toward my car when all of a sudden I heard two shots being fired.

"Oh my God!" I screamed then quickly ran for cover.

When three more shots rang out, I ducked down in front of an antique furniture store just before the window display's glass shattered all over me. It was at that point when I realized someone might've been shooting at me.

Shaking like a leaf, I prayed that I wouldn't get hit.

Moments later, I could hear a pair of tires screeching just as the shots instantly ceased.

Who the hell could want me dead, was all I could think about as I balled up on the street in a fetal position and cried.

Chapter 23

Marisol

"Your food is on the table!" Maria called to Denie for the second time over the intercom.

Wanting us to eat as a family, Carmen and I waited for Denie to join us for breakfast, but if she wanted to remain anti-social, then we were gonna start without her. Just as I was about to tell Maria to put her plate away, Denie finally came down-stairs. She looked a mess and seemed to be losing weight daily. She even reeked of odor and her hair was all over her head. With the same Betsey Johnson pajamas on for the past week, I wondered if she'd even taken a bath.

"I'm just gonna take my food up to my room," she said, grabbing her plate off of the table.

"Oh no, Denie, you're gonna sit down and eat with us as a family. I need to make sure you're eating because Maria has noticed that you always leave a plate full of food when she goes to clean your room."

"I appreciate your concern, but I'm not Carmen. I'm nineteen years old and I don't need…"

My appetite was instantly ruined when Denie started throwing up all over the place.

"Oh my goodness senorita, are you okay?" Maria asked as she ran to grab some towels to clean up the mess.

I stood up to help my daughter. "Carmen, stay with Maria. I'm going upstairs to help your sister get cleaned up."

Carmen nodded her head. "Okay Mommy. Feel better, Denie."

"I'm alright," Denie insisted.

"No, you're not. Come on," I responded as we made our way upstairs."

If there was anything I could've done to remove the pain from Denie's heart I would. It hurt me to see her in so much distress, and how she'd alienated herself from the world. I'd been worried sick about her ever since the incident at the hair salon. When Jermaine called and told me he'd found Denie laying on the sidewalk and that someone had shot up Georgia Avenue trying to get at her, my heart instantly stopped. To make matters worse, Denie had no idea who the person could've been. She didn't even get a good look at the car. That was the scary part.

One thing after another kept happening to Denie and I felt like her life was spiraling out of control by the minute. I'd worked so hard to try and get her past the Javier situation, and now this shit was a major set back. However, there was no way I was gonna allow anything to happen to my daughter, so I'd been keeping close tabs on her. It was my job as a mother to protect her, especially since her father wasn't shit. I hadn't even called him about the incident, and didn't have any plans on telling him. This was something I was gonna handle myself. For all I knew, it could've been because of something he'd done that caused this shit. I knew I'd chosen this crazy life for me and my family, but I probably would've had second thoughts if I'd known it would cost me their lives. Maybe it was time to get out the game. In the end, this shit wasn't worth it.

"Denie, what's wrong with you?" I asked as she sat down on her bed. "How long have you been feeling sick?"

"I don't know. It's nothing major. I just got dizzy for a second and became nauseated, that's all. Please just leave me alone. I need to change into something else."

"I'll back off, but just listen to me first. No matter what the past was with us and my faults, I love you and I always have if that means anything," I said, allowing my guilt to get the best of me.

Denie forced a slight smile. "I love you, too. I'm not mad at you. I understand more than you think I do."

"Well, help me understand what's going on with you then."

"It doesn't matter anymore. I'm just tired."

"You have to be strong, baby. I know that was a traumatic experience, but things will work out. Don't worry. Once I find out who did this, it's a wrap for them."

"I really don't feel like talking right now," Denie responded.

"Okay, can I just say one more thing and then I'll go?"

Denie slowly shook her head. "Yes, what is it?"

"I think if you try and work on your relationship with your father, you would be in a better place. I'm not gonna be dealing with him anymore, but that doesn't mean you shouldn't."

"What is it gonna take for you to see Rich for the animal he really is? He fucks up anything he touches. I used to be just like you and never understood why people only saw the worst in him until he hurt me," Denie informed.

"Well, your father really does love you and..."

"Look Marisol, I can't take it anymore. I need to tell you something."

"Denie, call me Mom. It made me feel good to hear you say that. I don't want to be Marisol to you anymore. I want to be your mother."

"Okay... Mom," she said with a smirk.

"That's better, now what's up?"

All of a sudden her smirk turned into a frown and she

broke down crying.

"I'm sorry I didn't listen to you."

I rubbed her back in a circular motion. "It's okay. I'm always gonna be here for you."

"Don't be mad, but I lied to you and I feel bad."

"Whatever you have to tell me I can take it, sweetheart. What's wrong?"

"Javier was telling the truth. I did tell him that Rich killed Uncle Carlos, because he did. He caught Lisa and Uncle Carlos together and that's what made him do it."

"Denie I know you're mad at your father right now, but it's no need to make things up because I know the truth. I know Lisa killed him."

Denie jumped up. "Stop being in denial and just hear me out. I'm so tired of Rich making you look like a fool. He killed Carlos, then covered everything up so that Uncle Renzo wouldn't kill us all. I'm sorry I didn't tell you after all you've done for me."

I stared at my daughter for a minute trying to process everything. "Denie, it's okay. I was going to kill Javier regardless, so don't feel like you have to carry that burden on your heart."

"I need you to believe me. It's the truth. Rich is a piece of shit!"

As my daughter cried and felt guilty for holding so much in, I finally saw Rich for the bastard that he really was. I guess it had to take the right person to allow me to see it. He was gonna pay for lying to me and taking my husband away from his kids. Trying to stay strong, I held back my true feelings.

"Well, baby, I hate a liar and I'll definitely get to the bottom of this. Just be easy. Don't worry about anything. I have it all under control. I just want to see my old Denie come back."

I wanted her to know that I was there for her no matter what.

"It's hard. There's just so much on my mind."

Not wanting to pry, I decided not to push her anymore.

But to my surprise, Denie suddenly opened up and started to talk. When she finally gave me details about the time she spent with Javier, I was appalled. At that moment, Jade's outburst at the funeral, became crystal clear in my mind. Now, it all made sense. She'd tried to send me a message, but I'd been too dumb to see it. All this time my daughter held the answers that I went through hell and high water to get. Finally, I knew the truth.

Even though deep down inside I always knew Rich killed Jade, Javier had still crossed the line by violating my nineteen year old daughter. Denie seemed to cry the most when she told me that Jermaine had given her some uncomfortable news about Javier, but wouldn't tell me anything else. As bad as I wanted to know what Jermaine said, I decided to wait until she was ready to open up. Denie was like a fragile flower now. At any moment she could fall apart, so I had to be overly delicate with her.

After a long heartfelt conversation, Denie and I promised to never keep secrets from each other. Although I knew she was still holding something back, I wasn't even sure if I was prepared for much more. At that point I needed some air and decided to go and get a mani-pedi. Along with the desperate nail pampering, I also needed a moment to digest all the information that had been exposed to me.

After I got out of the shower and put on some lotion, I decided to put on my green convertible maxi dress and a pair of flip flops. Tossing my sunglasses into my hot pink Louis Vuitton Alma bag, I grabbed my keys, then walked out of the door.

Today I decided to drive my BMW so I could let the top down and exhale. Once I got inside the car, I couldn't help myself. I needed to curse Rich out. As I dialed his number my blood boiled all over again. Of course he didn't answer the phone, so I decided to leave him a message.

"You bitch-ass nigga. I know you're ignoring my call, but it's all good. The jig is up muthafucka, you've been caught. I advise you to stay the fuck away from my house, and if not, you'll see what happens when you get here, you fucking punta!"

Taking a deep breath, it felt as though I had so much

more to say, but I had to plan this out carefully. As I waited for my iron gates to open, I looked in my rear view mirror and could see Carmen running out of the house with Maria chasing after her.

"Mommy, Mommy!" she yelled running toward my car.

"What the hell?" I quickly put my car in park and got out as Carmen ran down the pavement.

"I'm sorry, Miss Marisol. Carmen heard you tell Denie that you leaving, so she ran out after you crying."

"I wanna go with you, Mommy!" Carmen wailed.

"Carmen baby, I'll take you tomorrow. Mommy needs to have some time alone right now."

"But Mommy you don't ever take me anywhere anymore. I don't want to stay with Maria. I want to go with you," she whined.

Not wanting to disappoint my kids anymore, I quickly gave in. "Come on, Carmen get in," I said, opening the door.

Carmen was all smiles as she hopped inside moments later. She'd obviously played on my guilt, which ended up working in her favor. How could I argue with a five year old when she was telling the truth? Maybe a day with Carmen was what we both needed. Reaching down on the passenger side floor, I looked in my bag and got out my Chanel sunglasses and put them on.

"Mommy, where are my sunglasses?"

"Look in the glove compartment and get some."

Carmen held up a pair of pink sunglasses with heart shaped rims. "Mommy these aren't mines, these are Mia's."

"It doesn't matter, just put them on."

"No Mommy. She's gonna be mad at me."

I couldn't help but smile. "Baby, Mia is in heaven and she has a lot of sunglasses now, so she won't mind you wearing those, okay. She'll probably be happy that you're wearing them."

"Why can't I go to heaven and be with Mia and Daddy? Uncle Rich said a bad man hurt Daddy and that's why he had to leave and go to heaven."

"Ooh, Carmen, those glasses look pretty on your pretty face." I tried to change the subject when I felt my eyes well up with tears.

Her smile went from ear to ear. "Thanks, Mommy."

I couldn't believe that muthafucka had been talking to my daughter about Carlos. The more I found out about Rich, the deeper my hatred for him seemed to develop.

✶✶✶✶✶✶✶✶✶✶✶✶✶✶

Carmen and I ended up having a great day together, but since I still needed some time to myself, I told Maria to come and meet us at Woodmont Grill in Bethesda so she could take Carmen back home. As I walked Carmen to Maria's car, I locked eyes with a familiar face driving past the restaurant. It was Grady.

What the hell is he doing in town, I thought.

He hadn't called me in months, so I wondered what he was doing in D.C. Obviously he'd noticed me too because he held his hand up as he made a U-turn and I gave Carmen a kiss. By the time she and Maria pulled off, Grady pulled up. He had some chick in the car with him that gave me a '*who the fuck are you bitch*' look, but I decided to let it go. Little did she know, I could take him if I wanted, so she needed to calm the fuck down. After double parking, he jumped out of the car looking handsome as ever.

"What's up, babe?" he asked. His fine-ass got out and gave me a strong hug.

"Hey, Grady, what are you doing here?"

"I been in D.C. for a while. Man, I've been tryin' to get in touch with you for a minute now. Rich gave me your number, but every time I call your phone the shit is off".

I looked surprised. "What number did you call? Rich didn't tell me that you were trying to get in touch with me."

"I mean it's all good. I knew you were busy dealin' with

your daughter and all. Oh, I'm sorry to hear about your loss."

"Thanks Grady." I certainly didn't wanna talk about Mia. "So, what number did Rich give you," I asked as he went back to his Maserati to get his phone.

He was dressed really simple with a white tee, shorts and a pair of Gucci sneakers. With dark chocolate skin, he reminded me so much of Lance Gross. If I didn't have on my sunglasses I'm sure the bitch he had in tow would've been ready to beat my ass, because I was definitely checking him out. I couldn't hear what the chick was saying to him, but all I knew was her neck was rolling and by the end of their thirty second conversation her lips were pouting and her arms were folded. Maybe she could sense that me and Grady had fucked before. But, damn, it was a long time ago, when Carlos was alive. We were doing business one night in Houston, and one too many drinks had me on my back. We never discussed our one night since he feared Carlos would kill him, so it was water under the bridge right after we both came. But as horny as I was, I wouldn't have objected to taking another trip back down memory lane again.

"Here's the number right here," Grady said, handing me his Blackberry.

My eyebrows wrinkled. "This is Carlos' old number. Why would Rich give you this number?" For some strange reason, I had yet to disconnect Carlos' old phone service.

Grady shrugged his shoulders. "I don't know. He's been taken care of me. As a matter of fact I just left him a couple of hours ago."

"Oh really."

"Yeah. He said you wanted him to take care of things now since you were still dealin' with your loss. You seem shocked. Was the nigga lyin' or somethin'?"

I had to play it off. "Oh, no. That's exactly what I told him. Listen, put my number in your phone and give me a call for now on. I'm back so you can deal with me directly."

"Okay cool," Grady said, as he repeated the number back to me to ensure it was correct.

"Call me anytime, even if you get tired of that chicken head you got in the car."

"You know I will. Take care." He winked before walking back to the car and pulling off.

Smiling to hide my anger, I quickly ran back to my own car, then pulled out my phone. I was so pissed as I redialed Rich's number, my hands started to shake. Once again, I felt like a fool for trusting him. After finding out about the robbery and the Grady shit, now I knew who'd taken the ten grand that day. Here I was thinking that my most honorable business partner, Devin, had shorted me, and Rich's ass had been robbing me right up under my nose the entire time. There was no way I was going to allow him to get away with this shit.

"Yeah, man. You still wanna call and talk shit. Don't be leavin' me no messages like that," he answered as if my calls were irritating him.

"Let me tell you one fucking thing. As long as you live don't you ever fuck with my money, am I clear?"

"Who the fuck are you talkin' to, Marisol?"

"Your broke-ass. Are you so thirsty that you had to steal from me? What type of shit are you really on?"

"Who the fuck are you callin' broke?" Rich asked.

I could care less if I'd pissed him off. "You muthafucka. You're the only one on the phone, right? I can't believe you, Rich."

"What are you talkin' about, bitch? I didn't rob you."

"Correction, what I said was stealing from me. So, do you wanna admit that you were the one at the airport that day?"

The line was quiet for about three seconds. "Why would I admit to some shit like that when it's not true?"

"I didn't think your bitch-ass would. Who the fuck told you to fuck with Grady behind my back, and why would you give him Carlos' old number?"

"Man, fuck you and Grady. You all on that nigga's dick if you listenin' to what he sayin'."

"Actually, being on his dick is a whole lot better than

being on yours. I would take Grady over your little dick ass any day." I knew that comment would land as a low blow. Men hated when you talked about their manhood.

"Are you tryin' to be funny, bitch? I hope not since your pussy is some shit. I could care less if you ever get on my dick again. I got bitches, sex ain't ever been an issue for me. You're the one who keeps callin' beggin' me to come and fuck wit' you."

"Rich, please. You give yourself way more credit than you deserve. I can make myself cum muthafucka. My dildo does me just fine. There's nothing you can do to me that I can't do to myself so go fuck one of your whores. Just stay the fuck out of me and my daughter's lives."

"Bitch, that's my daughter! You come back in her life after me and Lisa do all the work and stake claim. You can't keep me away from my child."

"I won't have to work hard because she doesn't fuck with you and neither do I. I advise you stay the fuck away from me."

"Is that a threat?"

"Yes, it is."

I hung up on his ass before I exposed that I knew the truth about what he did to Carlos and Jade. Rich's days on this earth were definitely numbered.

Chapter 24

Marisol

More than ever, I was really through with his ass this time. Rich was dead to me as far as I was concerned and if it was the last thing I did, he was going to pay for thinking I was a joke. Not only was he playing me with that bitch Trixie the entire time, but now he was fucking with my money, and that's where I drew the line. I'd devised a plan for some major get back, and Trixie was gonna make it happen for me. No questions asked, she was gonna help me get this nigga. I'm sure she was surprised when I called a few hours earlier and told her we needed to meet at my house for a business meeting. She even tried to tell me that it wasn't a good idea, until I mentioned the word 'money'. Just like any other money hungry bitch, Trixie was quick to change her tune once she realized that I was willing to pay for her time. When anyone spoke about cash, Trixie would sell her soul to the devil. She would do anything for a coin which worked in my favor, but at the same time I knew that could also backfire and be dangerous. What I needed her to know was that I wouldn't mind getting rid of her ass if need be.

This shit was business…not personal.

Suddenly, the gate buzzed.

"I can't believe she's on time," I said, after looking into the monitor.

"Trixie?" I asked just to reconfirm.

"Yep. It's me," she responded.

After hitting the button to let her inside, I ran down stairs to open the door. When Trixie walked up a few minutes later, her ass was dressed like she was going out to a club somewhere even though it was only two o'clock in the afternoon.

Dolled up in an ivory ruffled dress that was probably a shirt, it fell off of her shoulder, and landed just above her ass. With her breasts spilling out the other end, she was way too sexy for what we were here to do. However, her red YSL platform sandals were to die for. One thing I could say about Rich, his bitches were always fly.

My past feelings toward Trixie had to be put aside since there was a job to be done. I needed her to come through, so I took a deep breath to give me some strength in order to deal with her ass. Sending Maria, Carmen and Denie out on a shopping spree, then to dinner and a movie, no one was scheduled to be home for a while, so I didn't have to worry about anyone knowing she was there. Since Rich and I were beefing, he definitely wasn't gonna be popping up either.

"Oh my goodness girl your house is off the chain," Trixie said with a huge smile. "I've never been out to Potomac before."

"Thanks, come on in," I replied as she admired my home.

Trixie looked in every direction as we walked through the foyer and made our way downstairs to the basement. You would've thought she was in a museum they way she complimented everything, from the paintings on the walls to the waterfall in my circular driveway.

With Denie confirming Jade's letter, it was evident that Rich killed my husband, and surprisingly I would've killed his ass too if I'd caught him fucking Lisa. But it was the way Rich went about the whole thing that made me upset. He might've even gotten a pass if he'd just been honest. The fact that he cried along with me on several different occasions, vowing to seek revenge on Carlos' killer was the fucked up part about all this. He was a liar, and couldn't be trusted after this, so now he had to be dealt with. Trixie was my trump card, and I wanted that bitch to deliver.

"Care for a drink?" I asked.

Trixie laid her purse on the bar. "Yes, what you got?"

"You want champagne, wine, white, or dark?"

"White all day. I'll have a Ciroq straight up."

I chuckled. "Damn, you trying to get fucked up, huh?"

"Girl, I need a drink with all the drama going on at my shop and with my oldest daughter, Toya. She went and got herself knocked up, and I'm not trying to be no damn grandmother."

To be honest I really wasn't trying to hear about her personal issues. I just wanted to get to the point of why she was here. I let her talk a little bit to bait her in, but the more shots we did, the more she told me her life story including the drama with Rich and her ex, Mike. It was obvious she missed him and had a little bit of animosity toward Rich, which would gladly work in my favor.

"So, why am I here? Why couldn't we do this over the phone?" Trixie questioned.

"Because this isn't the type of shit you do over the phone," I responded.

"Damn, so it must be serious, huh?"

"Very."

"So, what is it?" Trixie asked in a curious tone.

"I need you to help me get Rich."

Trixie seemed shocked. "Now, when you say get him, what exactly goes that mean?"

"What the fuck do you think it means?"

I let it be known that she had a timeline. It was important that we do this quickly, so games were not allowed. With me and Rich beefing he would probably be inclined to spend more time with Trixie, so her luring him to a certain location as opposed to myself would make him less suspicious. She was still pissed off that Rich was dealing with the both of us at the same time, but I told her to get over it. That shit was the Classic Rich that I'd known for years. The cheater in him would never die on his own, so I guess he needed a little help.

"So, how much we walking?" Trixie inquired.

"I'll give you fifteen thousand to start. Once you lure him to the designated spot, and this shit goes well, I'll give you another fifteen. If you keep your mouth closed, I'll hit you off with some more."

Trixie tried to play it off, but I knew her ass was excited. "Deal," she said without hesitation. "And why are you trying to lure him somewhere again?"

"Because, after our last conversation, let's just say he'll know that I'm up to something if I call talking sweet right now."

Trixie shook her head like she understood. "I see."

"Oh, by the way, Rich is money hungry like you, so he's not gonna budge for free. I'm gonna give you an extra ten thousand to throw his way in the beginning." When Trixie looked at me like she was offended by the name I called her, I displayed a slight grin. "Sorry."

After we were on our 5th shots of Ciroq, I went and got a bottle of Rose' Moet, popped it open then poured some into champagne flutes. I walked over and handed her a glass.

"Sorry for beating your ass." My words slurred due to me being tispy.

"It's all good. It's water under the bridge now. Let's toast to new friendships and letting bygones be...be...bygones," Trixie replied just as intoxicated.

"I'll toast to that," I said as we tapped glasses.

By the time we had two more glasses, now we were really drunk.

"What movies you got in here?" Trixie asked, walking into the theater room.

"I haven't been down here in a while. This is where Rich usually hung out. Let me see what's in here."

Grabbing the remote, I clicked it as the screen came down from the ceiling. Trixie was like a kid in the candy store. My theater was definitely a man cave and all around the entire room was either framed Basketball jerseys of Carlos' favorite athletes or his favorite movies.

"Gurl, I need me some shit like this in my house," she said in a ghetto demeanor.

"Make that shit happen with Rich and you'll have this and then some."

As I pressed play to see what was in the DVD player, it was a sex tape starring Pinky, Rich's favorite porn star. I should've known.

"Oh my goodness, I'm so sorry," I said, attempting to turn it off, but Trixie had other plans.

"Uh-uh. Don't turn it off. I love me some Pinky. Marisol loosen up some. Live a little."

She had no idea what I was capable of and I guess I had to show her. As I let the movie play I saw that she was becoming aroused due to the constant shifting in her seat. If she was trying to maintain her composure, the shit wasn't working. Standing up, I walked over and reclined her chair back, then started kissing her neck.

"You know I've been wanting you since the day you stepped foot in my shop," Trixie whispered as I licked her earlobes.

As I made my way back to her neck I pulled her dress down just enough to expose her pierced nipples. Flicking my tongue across her breast, I placed my hand under her dress, quickly finding out that she didn't have on any panties. When I used my index finger to play with her pussy, within seconds, Trixie moaned as if she was about to cum already. She must've been telling the truth about wanting me because before I could make my way inside her nest, she'd already pushed me down on the floor, pulled off my leggings and went to work. She sucked my moist pussy as if her life depended on it and surprisingly I loved every minute of it.

"Damn girl. You wanted this pussy, huh?" I asked as she began to tickle my clit with her tongue.

"You damn right," she said, nibbling on my pink lips.

At that point, I couldn't take it anymore. As the warm cum began to ooze out of my body, Trixie continued to flick her tongue causing my body to jerk out of control. However, as soon as I got myself together, I was determined to show her who was boss.

I stumbled to my storage closet and got my bag of tricks. Before I even got back in the room I strapped the dildo on. Once I walked back into the room she was ready, fully undressed. See, little did Trixie know, me and Carlos were swingers from time to time, but only when we were out of town or on vacation and I knew how to please a woman. My toy bag hadn't been put to use in a long time but tonight was special, it was operation take Rich down night, which caused for some desperate measures. I liked men, but a little swimming in the lady pond would never hurt a girl.

I'm about to fuck her better than Rich ever could, I thought to myself as I placed Trixie on her back and plunged the dildo inside.

With each powerful thrust, I tried to bang the shit out of Trixie's walls. When I pulled the dildo out, I made her suck it a little bit before putting it back inside of her drenched pussy. Moments later, Trixie got on top and started riding me until she finally came. She ended up cuming two more times before the night was over. A girl had to do what a girl and to do. With that bitch, Trixie, under my spell, now, I was sure it was a matter of time before Rich was lured into my trap. He had no idea that I could turn out any of his bitches to get what I wanted.

****

After a few hours with Trixie, I was tired as hell. I walked her out just before Maria and the kids were due to come back and then laid on the bed. As soon as I drifted into a good sleep, my cell phone rang and woke me up. *Unknown* popped up on my screen, which wasn't what I wanted to see. I definitely wasn't ready for the conversation I was about to have. Lorenzo was probably done with all of my promises that I was coming to see him for months and I was sure that he was calling to see why I had yet to arrive. I decided to answer and get it over with.

"I'll make sure I go see him after I take care of Rich so I can give him the information about Carlos he needs to be at peace," I told myself.

There was no need to listen to the recording so I pressed 0 so I could face my father-in-law.

"Hola, Papi."

"Marisol my darling, it's Armondo."

I was surprised. "Hey, Armondo, how have you been?"

"Not well. Something terrible happened last night. It's Lorenzo, he…" Armondo burst in to tears. This man was so tough, never in my life had I ever seen a weak side of him. For him to be crying I knew it only meant one thing.

"What's wrong with Renzo? Armondo, tell me what's wrong," I asked, praying my instinct was wrong.

"Lorenzo passed away. He had a heart attack in his cell last night. I don't know what to do. He was like my brother."

"Oh my goodness, he can't be dead," I said in disbelief.

"You need to come see me. There was something that he wanted you to know about..." the phone hung up.

Although I waited for him to call back, he never did.

There was no way to try and go back to sleep even if I tried. As my mind wondered, my guilt was overwhelming. After everything Lorenzo did for me, I could've visited him at least once. He deserved that. He deserved to know who'd killed his son. He deserved closure. Another Sanchez was gone. But the next one to go is the one who deserved to die.

Chapter 25

There was nothing that Ginger Ale could do to fight off this nausea that I was experiencing. It felt like I had a twenty-four hangover, but couldn't remember the last time I had a drink. After being sick for three days straight, I was on my way to my doctor's office in Georgetown, and couldn't help but think about all the shit I'd heard about Javier. I prayed to God that he hadn't given me anything that I couldn't get rid of or T-Roc for that matter. I know my mother wondered why I'd been so distant lately, but the possibility of being HIV positive constantly consumed my mind. Needing to move on with my life, I finally decided to just get everything over with by being tested.

After arriving at the doctor's office and checking in, I made myself comfortable in the waiting room, while catching up on the latest celebrity gossip from a *Sister 2 Sister* and *In Touch Weekly* magazine. The magazines I read also kept me ahead of the trends.

One day I'm going to have my own clothing line parading through these magazines, I thought to myself just before my name was called.

"Hi, are you Gardenia Sanchez?" the nurse asked.

"Yes." I threw my magazines back in my Gucci tote bag and followed the nurse through the door and into an examining room. As she started taking my vitals, the questions soon followed. I hadn't been to the doctor in so long, I was quite embarrassed.

"Wow, Gardenia your blood pressure is low. We'll need to take care of that right away."

"You can call me Denie."

"Okay Denie, what made you come in today."

The nurse was every bit of twenty-five years old, so I really didn't feel comfortable with telling her why I was there. All I could think of was, *suppose one day I bumped into her at a club or something.* The first time I caught her whispering, I would've been ready to whip her ass. As soon as she sensed my hesitation, her ass broke the ice.

"Denie, I've seen and heard it all so please know that nothing can surprise me. Your visit is strictly confidential. Remember we're here to help."

She's probably right, I thought. "Well, I've throwing up for a few days now even though I haven't even had an appetite. Then last night my legs started cramping really bad and I keep getting dizzy."

"That sounds like you might be dehydrated. We might need to get you started on an IV. When was your last menstrual period?" she asked.

"Oh my goodness, I've been under so much stress that I don't even remember."

"You know stress causes a lot of symptoms in the body, so that might be the cause of you not feeling well. Can you think around what month it was? Stand up and let me get your weight," she said.

Thinking back, I honestly couldn't remember. Damn, had it been that long?

"Umm…okay so it's the end of July and my period still

hasn't come on and I don't think it came in June either."

She wrote something down in my folder. "Are you using any contraceptives?"

"Sometimes."

"When was the last time you've had a complete exam and a pap smear?" she continued to drill.

"It's really been a while. Probably since I had an abortion years ago."

"Okay. I need you to get completely undressed and put this gown on with the opening facing the front. Also, I need you to fill out this paperwork. The doctor will be in soon."

"And what's your name?" I questioned.

"I'm Tomiko."

"Thanks for being so nice, Tomiko."

"No problem at all."

My heart raced as I sat on the examination table and waited for the doctor. I tried to play Scrabble on my I-Pad to keep myself occupied, but the nervousness just wouldn't go away. Finally, after twenty minutes slowly ticked by, the doctor came in. She was a young, black woman as well who looked fresh out of med school.

"Hello Ms. Sanchez. I'm Dr. Peyton." She looked in my folder. "I see that your blood pressure was low, but what else brings you here today?"

"Well, I was just telling the nurse that I've been experiencing nausea for a while now, along with dizziness and leg cramps, so I thought I would come in to see what was going on. She said it sounds like dehydration."

"Yes, those are some symptoms, so to be on the safe side, I'm going to start you on an IV. I understand that you didn't see your period this month and possibly last month. Is it a possibility that you might be pregnant?"

"Oh God, I hope not."

"I'm going to order some blood work to be drawn stat as well as a urine analysis."

"Umm. Is there anyway you can test for HIV, too?" I

questioned in a low tone. The walls in doctor offices were so thin sometimes, I didn't want anyone else to hear me.

"Yes…sure. You'll have to sign a HIV consent form though." Dr. Peyton seemed a bit concerned, but didn't pry.

"Okay. Are the results gonna come back today?"

"We have the rapid OraQuick tests in this office that only takes twenty minutes for the results. However, I'm also going to send your blood work for a thorough, standard HIV test that takes twelve days."

"Okay," I said worried as hell.

"Denie, everything is going to be okay," Dr. Peyton assured. "Once someone gets your blood and urine samples, I'll have all your testing done so we can see what's going on with you. In the meantime I want to tackle this possible dehydration so we're gonna move you into another room and get the IV started. Are you here with someone?"

"No, I'm alone."

"Well, would you like to call someone? It seems like you shouldn't be going through this alone."

"Thank you, Dr. Payton, but I really don't want to call anyone. I just wanna handle this on my own. My mother doesn't even know that I'm here. But just in case something goes wrong, I put her number at the top of the form. Her name is, Marisol Sanchez."

She nodded her head "Denie, is there something else bothering you?"

"I'm just worried." I could no longer hold it in, and started crying like a baby.

"You have to tell me what's going on so I'm able to help you."

"My ex passed away and I suspect that he was bi-sexual. I just want to be sure that he didn't give me anything."

"And that's why you asked about the HIV test, right?"

I nodded my head.

"Denie, you're not the first young lady that has come into my office worried about something like this. Here, wipe your face," Dr. Peyton said, handing me a tissue.

"I just want to get it over with."

"I understand. I'll go get Tomiko, now."

After Dr. Peyton walked out of the room, Tomiko came back in moments later and directed me toward the bathroom. Once I gave her my urine sample, we walked back into the room to start the blood sample. The last step was the IV. As soon as that was hooked up, I instantly felt better, and drifted off to sleep within minutes. When I suddenly starting dreaming about Juan, I jumped out of my sleep.

What the hell? I thought to myself.

It seemed so real. I hope me dreaming of my dead brother wasn't a sign that I was starting to be like that bitch Lisa or the fact that I might be joining him soon. After an hour of being hooked up to the IV, I immediately felt better, which was a good sign. Once I got off of the table, and got dressed, I met my doctor in her office.

"Okay, Denie your test results came back and you do have a couple of things going on. First, I want to let you know that unfortunately you are HIV positive."

It felt like my heart stopped. Why the hell did she have to just blurt it out like that? "What? Oh my God. Am I going to die," I said with my hand slightly over my mouth.

"Denie, with the medicine today, there are so many people who are able to live normal lives even after being diagnosed. Sure, you may have to take medication for the rest of your life, but HIV is no longer a death sentence. Now, we'll need to get you on some meds right away to keep the virus at a low level, so I'll make sure to prescribe you a combination therapy before you leave."

"Combination therapy?"

"That just means you'll have to take one than one anti-retroviral drug at one time. Taking a combination vastly reduces the rate of the virus becoming resistant."

The more Dr. Peyton spoke, the more lightheaded I became. I felt sick all over again.

"I also have to inform you that you are indeed pregnant. How far I'm not sure since you don't know you're last menstrual cycle. However, we would have to do a sonogram to get an accurate due date."

I looked at her like she was crazy. "Due date. I'm not having a baby in this condition."

"Denie, it is definitely your choice, but I'm still gonna give you some literature to read to educate yourself on everything we discuss today."

As Dr. Peyton went on and on, my mind went to another place. I couldn't believe it. There was nothing she could've said that would lift my spirits at that moment, so I basically stopped listening. Everything seemed to be a blur. After finally leaving her office, I walked to my truck like a complete zombie and cried my ass off.

How could I allow someone that I barely knew to destroy my life this way? I was so mad at myself for not listening to Rich and my mother. Getting so caught up for all the wrong reasons had now cost me my future. There were so many things going through my mind. I felt like my life was coming to an end and there was nothing I could do.

On top of all that, now I was pregnant. My luck has to be the worse. Thinking back, I hadn't seen my period this month or June, so I had to be at least eight weeks pregnant.

"Why me?" I said, banging the steering wheel.

After sitting in the parking lot for a little while feeling sorry for myself, I finally decided to leave. However, I didn't get far. I ended up driving to the bottom of the garage and parked again because I needed to cry as loud as I wanted to without anyone looking at me like I was crazy. If I wanted to yell I could and not have to apologize for being too loud. I ended up crying hysterically for at least twenty minutes before finally calming down. Realizing that I needed to go home, I pulled down my visor to get myself together.

"Oh shit!" I yelled once I saw a familiar face appear in my mirror.

"Hey, pretty pussy," T-Roc said as he put a knife to my throat.

"How the fuck did you get in my truck?"

"You made it so easy for me. You left your door unlocked. I've been followin' you for a while now and had to wait for the perfect time. After I tried to put a cap in your ass last week and didn't succeed, I had to think of somethin' else. I'm so clever, don't you think?"

With his breath reeking of alcohol and body order smelling like weed, I instantly wanted to vomit.

"Fuck you! What do you want from me?"

"You're the reason why the only man I ever loved is dead, so you deserve to die, too."

"I am going to die! Either you or the man you loved gave me HIV, so do whatever you want. I don't have anything to live for. You can kill me and this bastard I'm carrying."

"You're lyin'," he said as the knife went deeper into my throat. "I ain't give you shit and neither did Javier!"

"Get off me you fucking faggot!" I belted as T-Roc wrapped my ponytail around his hand.

"I'm going to kill your ass slowly."

"Who cares if you kill me? You would be doing me a favor. I don't want to have a baby by a down low faggot anyway."

At that moment, T-Roc made me get out of the truck. All I could think about was how I could get to the taser that I had under my seat. Since she knew I had to go out alone sometimes, my mother wanted me to carry some type of weapon at all times. She also told me to keep it in my purse. It was something else that I could add to my list of regrets for not listening to her.

"I hate you!" I screamed as he pushed me to the ground. I hoped someone would hear me.

"Not as much as I hate you," he replied then kicked me in my stomach repeatedly.

"Aighh, aighh!" I yelled out in pain.

"Since you don't want the baby, I'll help you get rid of it

right now. I'll cut this baby out of you," T-Roc said with a deranged expression.

As soon as he came toward me with the knife, I kicked him as hard as I could between his legs. As his body folded over, I tried to get away, but he managed to grab my leg. Kicking him several more times, when one of my kicks landed in his face, he just started to go crazy and ended up stabbing me in my thigh.

"Get away from me!" I screamed then tried to make it back to my truck. Due to the adrenalin, I guess I couldn't feel the pain.

After opening the door, I immediately went under my seat for the taser not realizing that he was right behind me.

"You came back for this," he said, snatching the device out of my hand.

As soon as T-Roc turned to throw the taser in another direction, I quickly reached back under the seat and pulled out the small .25 caliber gun. It was the other weapon my mother wanted me to carry.

"No, I came back for this," I said, letting off one shot in the middle of his forehead.

I didn't even have to watch his body drop. I knew he was dead.

Chapter 26

Rich

Sometimes I wondered if Marisol really wished she was a dude. The bitch really had balls sendin' me death threats, but if she really wanted to see me, she knew where to find me. I'm sure she could've at anytime put one of Uncle Renzo's Columbian goons on me, but her pride would never allow her to do that. She was the type of broad who had to prove a fuckin' point, so I had to keep my eyes open for her ass. Now that we were no longer fuckin' wit' each other, my money was really gonna be messed up. There was no way I could peel from her ass now. I couldn't wait to talk to Grady's ass. I'd specifically told that nigga not to mention shit to Marisol, and he'd ran his mouth like a bitch anyway.

Even though I still had Trixie in my corner, I knew that shit wasn't gonna work out. Bein' wit' her would take some ad-justments. She was a workin' class bitch, not someone wit' real paper, so her ass couldn't really offer me anything but some good sex. I could get good pussy from Honey.

"Damn, the more I think about it, maybe I should rekindle some real shit wit' Honey, especially since she obviously came up on some bread," I said to myself.

Just when I was formulatin' a plan in my head, Trixie broke my train of thought.

"Rich somebody's calling you from a 202 number."

"Who in the hell told you to touch my shit," I said snatchin' it out of her hand.

It was Lisa's mother and I damn sure wasn't in the mood for her bullshit. I answered the phone on edge ready to curse her ass out.

"Why are you callin' me? I'm tellin' you now I don't wanna hear about no credit card shit. "

"No, Rich, actually I was calling to thank you for replenishing the lilies on Lisa's grave. Not many people know that those are her favorite."

"Man, I ain't put no lilies on that bitch's grave. Shit, I ain't been there since you put her ass in the ground. Why are you playin' games? Get the hell up off my phone!" I yelled before hangin' up on her ass.

"Wow I thought I'd never see the day you called Lisa a bitch and actually meant it," Trixie said.

"Your ghetto-ass like that shit, huh?"

"Damn, is that how you're gonna talk to the woman who's taking you out today?" she asked.

"Man I gotta go out B-More today, I can't go nowhere wit' you."

"Rich, I've already planned a nice evening for us at the Borgata in Atlantic City."

"Atlantic City? Man, I don't have no money to ball like I want to up there. Do you know how much money I used to put on the crap table?"

"Well, I already reserved the room. Plus we go hang out at the 40/40 club tonight."

"Man I don't give a shit about no 40…"

"Before you say anything else, I have this for us to play with."

When she opened her robe and exposed her naked body, there were several hundred dollar bills taped to her stomach and thighs. She even had some on her nipples. I was so involved in my own head game that I didn't realize she was dolled up in her red bottoms tryin' to be sexy for me. Now, she definitely had my attention.

"And it's more where this came from," Trixie said, pulling a stack out of the robe pocket.

"Where the hell did you get all that bread from? Who the hell have you been trickin'?"

"You really know how to fuck up the mood. No worries. I'll find somebody else to go with me. Fuck you, Rich."

She tried to storm out of the room, but ended up trippin' over her own feet and fell. That shit was so funny.

"Damn babe, be careful. You don't wanna scar your knees up before you get to your date," I said followed by a huge laugh.

"I don't have a date! Why don't you just get out?" Trixie yelled.

"Oh, so you gonna do me like Marisol, huh?"

"Don't compare me to your other baby mother. I've dealt with that shit with you and Lisa for years and look whose still here. Don't forget, I'm always the one picking up the pieces. You've never given me the respect I deserve."

"Bitch, do you realize that me fuckin' wit' you is what caused my marriage to go south. You're the reason why she lost her mind. You runnin' your fuckin' mouth to that nigga, Mike, made him go after my wife and fuck my home up. You let that nigga raise my daughter as his own, and now you wanna talk shit to me."

"How long are you gonna throw that shit in my face? You chose to make me your side chick. You chose to fuck me without a condom and step out on your wife. And yes, I chose to fuck you to get ahead."

"Time for me to go. I don't feel like dealin' wit' another bitch who wants to talk shit."

I jumped up and started puttin' on my clothes.

"No Rich, wait. I'm sorry. Let's just go to Atlantic City and spend some time together. I can tell that you're stressed out."

"Naw, I'm good. You can take somebody else."

"Rich, please, I'm sorry I want you to go."

"I already told you that I don't have any money for that shit. Them people used to me droppin' thousands on the table. I can't roll up there wit' light pockets, I gotta rep to uphold!"

At that moment, Trixie ran to her drawer and pulled out another stack. "Here, take this. It's ten thousand. This should be enough to start you off with. If not, I'll give you more. Trust me, Rich it's gonna be worth your while. This trip could be your come up," she stated.

At that point, I could care less where she got the money. Now, Trixie was speakin' my language.

✶✶✶✶✶✶✶✶✶✶✶✶✶✶

Our ride to AC wasn't that bad. We got up there in less than three hours and Trixie gave me head for probably half of the travel time. That was the plus for me bein' the designated driver. When we arrived at the hotel around eight o'clock, the lobby was packed wit' so many chicks, I suddenly wished I was by myself. It felt like I'd brought sand to the beach. Trixie held onto me as we walked through the lobby to let it be known we were together, which pissed me off.

"Man, damn Trixie. Give me some fuckin' elbow room," I said, snatchin' away from her.

"You are so damn rude, Rich. Don't act like I don't exist."

"I'm just sayin' you ain't gotta be grabbin' on me and shit." I walked in front of her, so it looked as if we weren't to-gether.

"What's up, Trixie baby?" I heard some dude say.

Turnin' around, I could tell Trixie was flirtin' already by

the way her ass smiled and played wit' her hair.

"Hey, Darryl. How you been?" she asked.

"I'm just fine now that I bumped into you," he added.

After I realized they had no plans on endin' their conversation I gave that bitch the evil eye. Trixie had a phat ass and didn't mind showin' it off so bein' out wit' her was definitely goin' to be a problem. Moments later, she gave the dude a hug, then caught back up to me.

"That was my…"

I didn't give her a chance to explain before I smacked the shit out of her.

"Bitch, as long as you live, don't you ever embarrass me like that again."

I dropped her luggage right there by the front desk and walked off. I just had my Louie backpack, so I just strapped it on my back and rolled out as she called my name. Ignorin' her ass, I made my way to the Blackjack table first before I played craps.

After playing a couple of hands of Blackjack, I won two g's and then lost it all plus four more. Wit' only six g's left, I decided to make my way over to the craps table where I felt more comfortable. This rapper dude from ATL was at the table along with several broads who were standin' around sweatin' him and his chips. I walked up to the table like I had millions in the bank wit' swagger for days.

I could see the table minimum was only twenty-five dollars, but I figured I'd go hard by bettin' a hundred on every number.

"Gimmie all black chips," I said countin' out four thousand.

"Do you have a Borgota Black card, sir?" one of the pit bosses asked.

"I don't have it on me, but you can look me up in the system," I said, handin' him my license and checkin' out the chicks who were on ATL's dick.

Once all the shit was taken care of, and the dealer handed

me my chips, it was on.

Sittin' three hundred dollar chips down in front of me on the pass line, I was ready to win big. Once this crazy lookin' Asian man rolled the dice and an eleven came up, I instantly yelled.

"That's what I'm talkin' about!" I said, once the dealer slid three additional hundred dollar chips in my direction. I'd won that fast.

Although I lost when a few of the other shooters crapped out, I ended up gettin' my luck back when ATL started rollin'. After winnin' a few hard eights bets, you couldn't wipe the smile off my face. But when I placed two hundred on snake eyes and won, the entire table screamed. Of course I began talkin' even more shit.

"Let's get this mufuckin' money!" I told everybody. "Scared money don't make no money, baby. Come on ATL!"

Everyone looked at me like I was crazy, but I didn't give a fuck. We were killin' the Borgota. By the time I was up twenty g's them same bitches who didn't even look at me before started hawkin'.

"Can I be your lucky charm," this fine-ass dark skinned chick flirted.

She looked just like Lauryn Hill with a Colgate smile. Before I could even respond a familiar voice called out.

"Oh no sweetheart he's good."

It was Trixie's hatin'-ass. I had to play nice even though I was winnin' because just in case I lost, she had the rest of the bread, so I just winked at her. I guess she'd forgotten about me smakin' the shit out of her a few of hours ago.

"Double shot of Ciroq…straight," I told the waitress walkin' around for drink orders.

"Make that two please," Trixie added.

Even though she'd pissed me off earlier, I couldn't help but notice how good Trixie looked in her red Dolce dress. I'd bought her that dress years ago and she still looked damn good in it.

Casinos were smart. They pumped you wit' free liquor because the tipsier you got, the more you gambled, which is exactly what happened to me. Once the waitress brought us those drinks, I ended up downin' three more.

As the dice rolled, my chips kept stackin'. Trixie stayed by my side as my cheerleader and made sure I kept a drink in hand. She was probably tryin' to get me fucked up so she could take advantage of me that night, and I was down for the cause. At this point I was up fifty g's and the shit felt good.

Maybe this is a good breakin' point so that I can start fresh tomorrow, I thought to myself.

"Baby I'm twisted, shit. I need to stop before I start losin'," I whispered to Trixie.

I didn't want people to get mad once I rolled out, but then again that wasn't a bad idea. The streets were always watchin' and I wasn't tryin' to get jacked out here.

"Let's go, then," Trixie replied.

Trixie tried to get me to put my chips in her purse, but that shit wasn't about to happen. I ended up puttin' them all in my backpack, so they could be in my possession. As we walked toward the elevator I was so fucked up I started stumblin' a little bit.

"Shit, I'm about to go to the room and lay down for a little while."

"I don't want to go to the room, Lets hang out," she nagged.

"Naw, man you can cancel that 40/40 idea cuz I'm not tryin' to do no hot shit! Did you see all them dudes from up top around the table? I'm not tryin' to get robbed out of town."

"But Rich I wanna fuck you on the beach. Can we please go, my pussy is drippin' wet," she said, grabbin' my dick.

I looked around to make sure no one was watchin'. "Bet."

Trixie knew how to get me because before I knew it we'd walked outside, got in a cab and made our way over to the boardwalk. When we hopped out a few minutes later and made

our way onto the sand, Trixie took her five inch Gucci heels off
and sashayed in front of me. I followed behind her ass like a
newly trained puppy.

"Come on, Rich let's go all the way over here so no one
can see us. I ain't trying to get locked up for indecent exposure,"
Trixie said.

"Aight. Whatever your freaky-ass wanna do. I want you
to fuck the shit out of me, because I'm too drunk to do anything," I responded. "Bitch, stop walkin' so fast."

"I'm not walking fast. Call me another bitch and I'll go
back to the room and play with my pussy instead of giving you
some."

"Okay, I'm sorry. How much longer?" I said, lookin'
around. "Man ain't nobody all the way down here." It felt like
we'd walked to the end of the earth.

We must've been far enough because all of a sudden
Trixie started to strip as she walked in front of me. My manhood
was definitely at attention as I watched her play wit' herself
when she stopped and faced me. I was ready to fuck the shit out
of her when all of a sudden somethin' hit me in the back of my
head.

"Get da fuck on da ground!" a strange voice yelled

Chapter 27

Marisol

Fucking with Rich had turned my life upside down. All because of a vendetta that Javier had against him, it was eventually gonna cost Denie her life. HIV positive is all I could think about as I looked at this nigga with his head buried in the sand.

"Keep ya head down!" I yelled in my Jamaican accent as I put the gun to Rich's head.

"Trixie, man, I told you them muthafuckas were watchin' us!" Rich shouted.

He thought she was laying right beside him. He also was the only one who didn't know what was about to go down. I threw the handcuffs to Trixie.

"Handcuff him," I ordered Trixie as her naked body climbed over to Rich and did as she was told. She handcuffed him just the way we planned. Right foot to left hand and left foot to right hand.

"Man, just take the chips in my bag," Rich slurred.

"I don't want ya money, bumboclot. I want ya life and ya gurl!" I belted. I just wanted to see what he was going to say about the girl part.

He was so drunk he couldn't even decipher my voice anyway as I continued in my accent.

"You can have that bitch. She ain't my girl," Rich responded. "Man, I just ain't tryna die out here."

At that point, I had to hit him in his head again. He deserved it just because I could see the hurt in Trixie's eyes. However, as much as I felt sorry for her, I also knew that I couldn't leave any witnesses. I was now at a point of no return. I pointed the gun in her direction.

"Lay down," I ordered to Trixie. This time I didn't bother with the accent.

"What are you doing?" she asked in disbelief.

Ignoring her, I walked over to Rich so he could see my face. I wanted him to look me in my eyes. "So, how does it feel? You know being robbed...by a Jamaican?"

"You bitch, you set me up!" he roared.

"Marisol, this wasn't the plan!" Trixie yelled.

"Sorry, Trixie, but your services are no longer needed." I pulled the trigger of my .9mm, shooting Trixie right in the head.

"Awww shit! What the fuck is your problem? Why man, why? All over Grady! You gonna kill my baby mother over that short shit!" Rich talked more and more shit. "Why did you kill her, man?" he yelled again.

Even though Rich was in such a drunken rage, he wasn't gonna live to suffer from his hang over.

"Wow, it's interesting that you would sit here and cry over the same person that got you here. Not to mention, you were about to sell her out earlier. You're more pathetic than I thought."

"Fuck you. You're the reason why...you're the reason."

"What the hell is your drunk ass talking about?"

"You are like Eve, the forbidden fruit. I should've never fucked you a long time ago."

"Admit it Rich!" I yelled in his face. "Admit what you did, you fucking punta. You robbed me! It was you all along!"

"I don't know what you talkin' about."

"You're are gonna die anyway so tell me. Tell me why. I would've given you anything. Why did you have to rob me? Admit it Rich. Make it right before you die. Make it right with me. I found my luggage in your mother's house. Do you know how hard it was to hold this in? I wanted to kill you right then and there. Just keep it the fuck real. Be a man and face your lies."

"Why should I satisfy the women who killed my son? Why should I give satisfaction to the bitch that fucked up my life? You turned my baby against me."

"You're not gonna put Juan's blood on my hands and don't you dare bring Denie into this! There's nothing that you can do to make me feel guilty for getting rid of your ass. I've let you live too long as it is."

"Bitch, you damn right I robbed you. I needed the bread and you had it. I knew you probably would'a gave me this shit if I asked, but it felt better to take it."

"But I loved you."

"Marisol, you don't know what love is. You always actin' like you're so loyal, but your loyalty ain't to nobody but your muthafuckin' self. You ain't no real mother. Maria might as well be those kids' mother. You the reason why Mia died. After I'm long gone always remember those words," he slurred.

The more he spoke, the more furious I became. His words stung. Tears streamed down my face as I stood over him with my gun pointing straight at his chest. He continued with his badgering and for a minute I was paralyzed and couldn't respond.

"I can't believe you just said that."

"Fuck you. You turned my daughter against me and you killed my son. Now you wanna play victim. You did it. You set him up, admit it."

"No, I didn't, but his hot-ass deserved to die. Snitches get stitches. That muthafucka fucked us up from getting real money. We were ready to retire from the game before his ass got the Feds involved," I said. "You did it, didn't you? You killed Carlos."

"You damn right I killed him. He died right in my wife's pussy. All this time I've been feelin' sorry for killin' Los. Now it's off my chest, I did it. So, what you gonna do now, bitch. Go ahead and kill me," he taunted.

"How could you, he loved you!" I hollered, then released the first bullet that landed in his shoulder.

"Aighhhh!" Rich yelled as the iron burned through his skin.

As I stood over him with the gun I cried and thought of every mistake that I'd made. If we'd never had sex half of the problems that existed wouldn't be a factor. He was right. I was Eve. I made him eat the forbidden fruit and all of the secrets and lies I lived to cover up my guilt wouldn't have been an issue if I'd never done the unforgiveable. I'd deprived my kids of a healthy non-violent life. But now all that was about to change.

"This one's for Denie and this one's for Carlos," I said, emptying the last two bullets into Rich's head.

Chapter 28

Marisol

Seven months later

Who would ever thought I would be a grandmother this young, I thought to myself as I drove home in the rain from Washington Hospital Center.

Denie had delivered a healthy baby boy. As I watched the windshield wipers fight the down pour, I said a prayer to myself to show my appreciation for a healthy baby. God answered our prayers and blessed Denie with a HIV negative son that we named after Carlos. He was what I needed to make me decide to give up the street life. Even though I was having a home built in Sarasota, Florida for us to live in, I still had to make sure my grandson had a fabulous nursery until then. I had Jaleel, the guy who'd done all of the paintings in my house, to come do a jungle mural on the wall of the baby's room. The color scheme we chose was chocolate brown, blue, and green. We added animals throughout the room including a life size giraffe and lion to bring it all together. The glider we'd ordered from Great Beginnings had arrived earlier that week just in time, so when Denie came home she would be comfortable.

Only one more day until Denie and the baby come home.

The more I thought about it, I got extra excited. It killed me that visiting hours were over and I had to leave because I was so in love with Baby Carlos and I missed him already. I couldn't help myself so I decided to call Denie's hospital room.

"Hey Denie. What's my baby doing?"

"Oh my gosh, he's doing the same thing he was doing before you left fifteen minutes ago…sleeping. I'll call you when he wakes up."

"Alright. Give him a kiss for me."

"Okay bye," she said, rushing me off the phone.

Sometimes I wondered if Denie's attitude was due to the hormones while she was pregnant. During her pregnancy I tried to be as supportive as possible so she could carry my grandson to term. But I often wondered if she resented me for killing Rich. No matter how much Denie acted like she hated him, I knew a part of her still loved him. As crazy as it sounds, I still had a place in my heart for him as well…no matter how much I tried to convince myself otherwise.

As I pulled up to the iron-gate to my house, I pushed the remote on my visor but the gate wouldn't open. Dreading getting wet, I got out of the car, unlocked the gate with the emergency key in case of a power outage and manually opened the heavy gate with my hands. By the time I made it back inside the car, I was soaked. It looked like I'd been in a wet t-shirt contest from the way my clothes were sticking to me. Instead of pulling into the garage, I decided to just park in front of the house in the circular driveway. I wanted to make sure we had power since the storm seemed to be getting worse.

When I walked into the house, there was no electricity, just as I thought. Times like these made me wish there was a man around the house. Since there wasn't anyone home, I decided to take my clothes off in the foyer so I wouldn't track water throughout the house. Feeling my way around until I made it to the kitchen, I got a flash light so I would be able to see.

When I walked upstairs and headed toward my room, there was a flicker of light in the nursery that caught my attention. I knew that no one was home and Maria had taken Carmen to her gymnastics practice. When I walked back to see where the light was coming from, I noticed there was a candle lit.

Why the hell would Maria leave a candle lit if no one was gonna be home all day, I fussed at her in my head.

Blowing the light out, I grabbed the flashlight and headed back to my room. As soon as I walked through the door, all of a sudden the T.V. came on by itself. Thank God the power was back on. I turned on the light and looked through my drawer for some underwear and a tank top to wear to bed. As I turned around to go in the bathroom to take a shower, I was shocked at what I saw. My heart instantly started pounding so fast, I thought a heart attack was near. Was I tripping?

"Oh my God, Juan is that you."

"I'm not a ghost. Surprise bitch," he said, aiming his gun at me.

"I can't believe it…you're alive." He'd grown a beard and had put on at least thirty pounds. He also had a dent on the side of his head that sorta reminded me of 50 Cent's gunshot wound.

"No shit."

"Why are you pointing that gun at me?"

"Where should I begin? The last time I checked you set me up for Renzo, tortured my mother while she battled with her mind, and lastly you killed my father."

"I didn't set you up, Juan. I cared about you. What were you thinking when you thought you could take down Lorenzo?"

"With all the money he had, I guess he couldn't buy a new heart. Heart problems a motherfucker, huh," Juan smirked. "I guess after I sent him that letter from you, about how you were out here living with Rich as a family and how you'd forgiven him for killing Carlos, that fucked him up."

"Juan, do you know what you've done? If the

Columbians find out, there's no witness protection that's gonna protect you."

"Fuck witness protection. I don't need that anymore, especially now that Armondo is dead, too. That nigga got shanked in jail, so now I'm good. Me, my sister and my nephew are gonna be alright."

"Denie would never forgive you if you kill me. I'm all that she has," I replied.

"If that's the case, ask Denie how long she knew I was back. How did you think I knew you were on your way back home from the hospital?"

My eyes enlarged. "She wouldn't dare. She's my daughter, you hot muthafucka. There's no way she would ever hurt me."

"She was my sister first. Do you think Denie really forgave you for leaving her at birth for some dick? You chose Carlos over your daughter and she's never forgiven you for that."

"I don't believe you. I was there for my daughter when it mattered and I'm going to be there for my grandson Baby Carlos. Denie needs me, she's sick."

"She's sick because her being here in your house caused her to meet the dude who turned her life upside down. Baby Carlos, huh? Is that what she told you?" Juan smiled. "Denie is getting good. My nephew was named after me and my father, Juan Sanchez."

I laughed, too. "Juan you really are delusional…just like your mother."

His smile instantly turned into a frown. "Marisol, I'm tired of talking to you. I'm tired of looking at your face, I'm tired of hearing your voice," he said, raising the gun a little higher like he was trying to get the perfect aim.

"Juan wait, please don't."

"I'm sorry, Marisol but you're the only one left that I would have to watch my back for."

"But Juan I never had beef with you."

"Bitch, you killed my father. I looked forward to the day

me and him could rebuild our relationship and you ruined it for me. So…stop fucking whining."

"But Denie needs me. Juan, you can't take care of her and the baby."

"Denie will be fine, Marisol. Now, it's time for you to go."

Blop, blop, blop. I fell to my knees as the bullets pierced through my skin and fire burned through my body. My vision of Juan faded quickly and finally I was at rest. Finally I was away from the drama. I was going home to be with my husband and my daughter.

Chapter 29

Juan

Damn, I never been a killer, but I couldn't believe how easy it was for me to put three bullets into Marisol's chest. I aimed straight for the heart. Once I knew I didn't have to worry about Uncle Renzo any longer, I was determined to come back and take my sister out of that dead end environment. It just hurt that I couldn't come back sooner to save my mother. I hated that she thought I was dead, but in order to get Renzo and Armondo behind bars, I had to disappear. I could only imagine how bad she sobbed at the casket during my so-called funeral. With the casket never opened, I had no idea whose body was actually inside. It's crazy what those fucking Feds could pull off. After Renzo and his goons tortured, pistol whipped and even shot me, when I finally woke up, I was on a farm out in North Carolina somewhere to heal, while awaiting Renzo's trial. See, even though Renzo shot me in the head, I managed to survive. I'm just lucky they were dumb enough to leave me in the hotel room instead of dumping my body at some deserted location. I guess it was meant for me to be here. Now, I understood why my mother and father wanted more for me and Denie. They wanted to give us what they didn't have, and that was peace.

Walking closer to my mother's grave I became extremely choked up. The last time I was here I put lilies on her grave as a peace offering. I wanted her to know how sorry I was for not being there. How sorry I was or putting her through so much pain. Why couldn't she just hold on long enough until I left the witness protection program?

I wish I could just hug her one more time, I thought to myself as I replaced the old flowers with the new ones.

"Hey Ma. I just want to let you know that I took care of Marisol. I'm sure you know how much she deserved it. Now, it's only me and Denie. We promised to be there for each other just like you always wanted. We're also done with the street life. We need a fresh start so we're moving to Florida. The house Marisol built is actually in Denie's name, so we have some-where to go…somewhere to start over. You would be proud of me, I plan on taking golf lessons when I get out there. I'ma be on some Tiger Woods type shit." Rubbing my hand across her tombstone, tears started to trickle down my face. "Well, I gotta go pick up Denie and my little nephew. He's such a beautiful lit-tle boy. I'll have to bring him to see you one day. We actually decided to take care of Carmen, too. Can you believe that was Denie's idea? I guess she's finally growing up. I love you, Ma and don't worry about us anymore. You can finally rest. Life is gonna be good now."

Coming Soon

V.I.P.

CONFESSIONS OF A Groupie

A NOVEL BY
AZAREL

In Stores Now!!

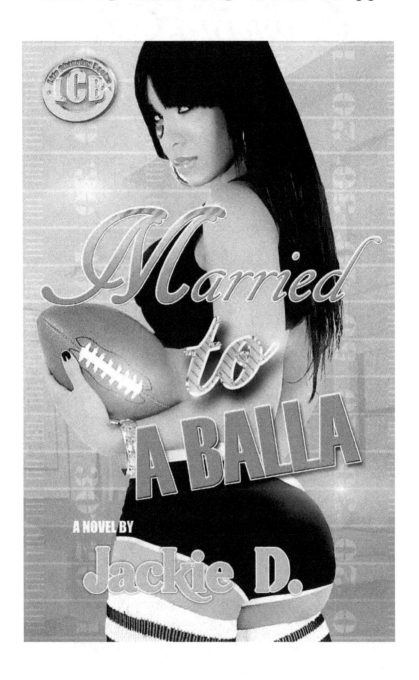

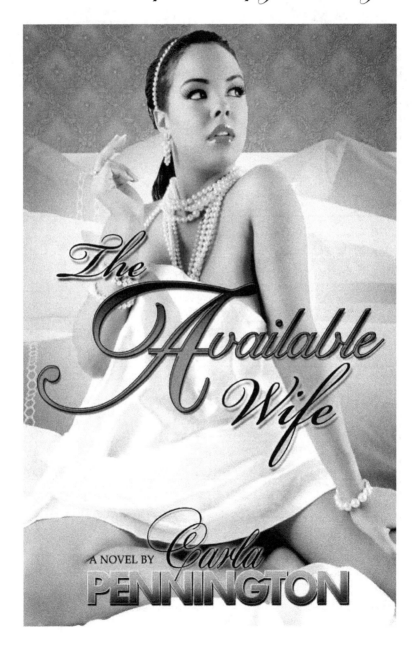

Pick Up a Copy Today

The Available Wife

A NOVEL BY Carla PENNINGTON

MAIL TO:
PO Box 423
Brandywine, MD 20613
301-362-6508

FAX TO:
301-579-9913

ORDER FORM

Ship to:		
Address:		
City & State:		Zip:

Date: _____   Phone: _____

Email: _____

Make all money orders and cashiers checks payable to: **Life Changing Books**

Qty.	ISBN	Title	Release Date	Price
	0-9741394-2-4	Bruised by Azarel	Jul 05	$ 15.00
	0-9741394-7-5	Bruised 2: The Ultimate Revenge by Azarel	Oct-06	$ 15.00
	0-9741394-3-2	Secrets of a Housewife by J. Tremble	Feb-08	$ 15.00
	0-9741394-8-7	The Millionaire Mistress by Tiphani	Nov 06	$ 15.00
	1-934230-99-5	More Secrets More Lies by J. Tremble	Feb-07	$ 15.00
	1-934230-98-7	Young Assassin by Mike G.	Mar-07	$ 15.00
	1-934230-85-2	A Private Affair by Mike Warren	May 07	$ 15.00
	1-934230-94-4	All That Glitters by Ericka M. Williams	Jul-07	$ 15.00
	1-934230-93-6	Deep by Danette Majette	Jul-07	$ 15.00
	1-934230-96-0	Flexin & Sexin Volume 1	Jun 07	$ 15.00
	1-934230-92-8	Talk of the Town by Tonya Ridley	Jul-07	$ 15.00
	1-934230-89-8	Still a Mistress by Tiphani	Nov-07	$ 15.00
	1-934230-91-X	Daddy's House by Azarel	Nov 07	$ 15.00
	1-934230-88-X	Naughty Little Angel by J. Tremble	Feb-08	$ 15.00
	1-934230847	In Those Jeans by Chantel Jolie	Jun-08	$ 15.00
	1-934230855	Marked by Capone	Jul 08	$ 15.00
	1-934230020	Rich Girls by Kendall Banks	Oct-08	$ 15.00
	1-934230839	Expensive Taste by Tiphani	Nov-08	$ 15.00
	1-934230762	Brooklyn Brothel by C. Stecko	Jan 09	$ 15.00
	1-934230869	Good Girl Gone bad by Danette Majette	Mar-09	$ 15.00
	1-934230804	From Hood to Hollywood by Sasha Raye	Mar-09	$ 15.00
	1-934230707	Sweet Swagger by Mike Warren	Jun 09	$ 15.00
	1-934230677	Carbon Copy by Azarel	Jul-09	$ 15.00
	1-934230723	Millionaire Mistress 3 by Tiphani	Nov-09	$ 15.00
	1-934230715	A Woman Scorned by Ericka Williams	Nov 09	$ 15.00
	1-934230685	My Man Her Son by J. Tremble	Feb-10	$ 15.00
	1-924230731	Love Heist by Jackie D.	Mar-10	$ 15.00
	1-934230812	Flexin & Sexin Volume 2	Apr 10	$ 15.00
	1-934230740	The Dirty Divorce by Miss KP	May-10	$ 15.00
	1-934230758	Cheefde Boyz by C.J Hudson	Jul-10	$ 15.00
	1-934230766	Snitch by VegasClarke	Oct 10	$ 15.00
	1-934230690	Money Maker by Tonya Ridley	Oct-10	$ 15.00
	1-934230774	The Dirty Divorce Part 2 by Miss KP	Nov-10	$ 15.00
	1-934230170	The Available Wife by Carla Pennington	Jan 11	$ 15.00
	1-934230774	One Night Stand by Kendall Banks	Feb-11	$ 15.00
	1-934230278	Bitter by Danelle Majette	Feb-11	$ 15.00
	1-934230299	Married to a Balla by Jackie Davis	Mar 11	$ 15.00
			Total for Books	$
		Shipping Charges (add $4.95 for 1-4 books*)		$
		Total Enclosed (add lines)		$

CPSIA information can be obtained
at www.ICGtesting.com
Printed in the USA
LVHW082354201019
634794LV00006B/154/P